BIKINI JONES VS. THE SEA MONSTERS

PATRICK THOMAS

PADWOLF
PUBLISHING

PADWOLF PUBLISHING INC.
WWW.PADWOLF.COM
www.facebook.com/Padwolf

www.patthomas.net

BIKINI JONES VS. THE SEA MONSTERS

cover art by Patrick Thomas3

ISBN 978-1-890096-96-99-1

First Printing. Printed in the USA

My blow hadn't bothered her. When she rushed me again, I was ready. I placed two fingers behind her ear and spun her in a circle, flipping her onto her back. I stomped my heel on her solar plexus, pivoted, and kicked her kneecap inwards to dislocate it.

She might be ten times as strong and three times as fast but her patella still worked the same way as a non-powered one. Knocking it out of joint meant she wasn't going to be able to stand, at least for the moment. Plus the pain would distract her while I spun again and rammed three fingers up into her brachial plexus through her sweaty and thoroughly unpleasant armpit. I maneuvered between her super-dense muscle to hit the nerves. She wouldn't be using that arm for a couple of hours.

Meanwhile across the yard, Blitz Meg wasn't smirking anymore. People used to being the strongest person in the room often couldn't figure out how to react when dealing with an opponent who out-muscled them.

The Nazi jumped on the shark woman's shoulders and tried to choke her out with a scissor kick, but her legs weren't long enough. Matoka just threw herself back onto the concrete, using the Nazi to cushion her impact.

I was on my way to help the shark woman end her fight quicker when I noticed red dots appear on her, then looked down and saw one on my chest. It was more than a little disturbing that neither of the racist duo was lit up by laser sites. It gave weight to my idea that one or more of the guards might have been paid to help kill us as well.

"Matoka, don't move. The guards have you in their sights."

The shark woman ignored me and turned to stare at the guards on the catwalk. "I doubt the bullets are going to do more than annoy me."

The shark woman's mutated form sported extremely dense muscle, but that was a far cry from being bulletproof. It was the bad kind of interesting that rifles were in use when the guards for the powered cell block had weapons available that were much more effective and far less lethal.

I slowly raised my hands over my head in the universal gesture of "I give up." Annie Bellum hopped onto her good leg toward me and Blitz Meg leapt off the ground at my midsection.

Moving to defend myself would give a corrupt guard a reason to shoot me but doing nothing ended with me being killed by the super-strong racists.

I had to try to manage both. Without dropping my arms, I twisted to avoid the Nazi human torpedo but stopped short as a firehose-sized stream passed on either side of me. The streams weren't water.

They were made of worms.

That's it. This was how I was going to die. The Queen of Worms was going to have her revenge.

BOOKS BY PATRICK THOMAS

The Murphy's Lore series
TALES FROM BULFINCHE'S PUB
FOOLS' DAY
THROUGH THE DRINKING GLASS
SHADOW OF THE WOLF
REDEMPTION ROAD
BARTENDER OF THE GODS
NIGHTCAPS
EMPTY GRAVES
THE MUG LIFE

Murphy's Lore Startenders
STARTENDERS
CONSTELLATION PRIZE

Murphy's Lore After Hours Universe:
Terrorbelle:
FAIRY WITH A GUN
FAIRY RIDES THE LIGHTNING
TERRORBELLE THE UNCONQUERED
Agent Karver:
RITES OF PASSAGE *(with John French)*
DEAD TO RITES
Hell's Detective:
LORE & DYSORDER
BULLETS & BRIMSTONE
 (with John French)
THE CASE OF THE MOON MANIAC
 (graphic novel with Blair Webb)
Hexcraft:
BY DARKNESS CURSED
BY INVOCATION ONLY
Soul for Hire:
GREATEST HITS

Xiles:
EXILE & ENTRANCE

Bikini Jones:
BIKINI JONES VS. THE
BRAINNAPPERS FROM OUT SPACE
BIKINI JONES VS THE SEA MONSTERS
BIKINI JONES VS THE EMPEROR OF
PLANET Z

The Jack Gardner Mysteries
THE ASSASSAINS' BALL *(with John L. French)*

Grifein, Batsquatch, & Dingbat:
CRYPTID FIGHT CLUB

Dear Cthulhu Series
HAVE A DARK DAY
GOOD ADVICE FOR BAD PEOPLE
CTHULHU KNOWS BEST
WHAT WOULD CTHULHU DO?
CTHULHU HAPPENS
CTHULHU EXPLAINS IT ALL

Mystic Investigators series
MYSTIC INVESTIGATORS
MEAN STREETS
ONCE MORE IN CRIME omnibus
 by Patrick Thomas & Diane Raetz
SHADOWS & BRIMSTONES omnibus
 by Patrick Thomas & John L. French

Agents of the Abyss:
FRANKENSTEIN: MONSTERS OF
THE ABYSS *(with John L. French)*
STARING INTO THE ABYSS: *Editor*

Playworlds:
AS THE GEARS TURN:
 Tales of Steamworld

YA:
THE WILDSIDHE CHRONICLES OMI
(contributing author)

Anthologies as co-editor
NEW BLOOD *(with Diane Raetz)*
CAMELOT 13 *(with John L. French)*

Writing as Patrick T. Fibbs
YA
EMOTIONAL SUPPORT NIGHTMARE

Middle Readers:
UNDEAD KID DIARIES:
 OVER MY DEAD BODY
BABE B. BEAR MYSTERIES:
 BAD HAIR DAY
JOY REAPER CHECKS OUT
Younger Readers:
Ughaboos picture books
5 SILLY MONSTERS JUMPING
 ON POOR ZED
ON TOP OF A YETI
SOGGY GOES TOT THE BEACH
 an Ughaboos early reader
FUSCHIA: THE MERMAID WHO
 LOVED PINK

For Erin & Colin

1

You never expect a shark attack, especially when it happens on dry land. On Fifth Avenue near 37th Street in Manhattan, to be precise.

No, the streets of New York hadn't been flooded by a lovesick mutant mermaid trying to film a viral music video again. Nor were there any tornados hurling hungry sea life through the air.

To be fair, it wasn't a traditional shark. For one thing, she had legs and arms. For another, she could talk. Scream in fact.

Her first roar was filled with anger as she leapt on top of the limousine and tore the roof off as easily as I would peel a banana. Her second scream was followed by her yanking the Mayor out of his now convertible limousine. His screams joined with hers. Understandable, since she held him so that his head was in front of her mouth. It should surprise no one that it was filled with many large and sharp teeth.

"Our babies are dying because of you!" the shark woman roared.

I gave the Mayor credit. After a moment of facial calisthenics, he put an expression on his blood-drained face that screamed interest. Nowhere near the volume of the shark lady, of course.

"Madame, I assure you I would *never* harm a baby."

"Maybe you didn't dirty your own hands, but you're letting Voxamatik Corporation ignore your surface laws and dump toxic waste into the river. You know who lives in the East River?"

The Mayor took a guess. "Fish?"

The shark woman's lips parted wider, making her teeth seem even larger. "You know who else lives there besides fish? The Mano!" The mayor slipped and looked confused. "Us shark people! And whatever Voxamatik is dumping is making all of our children deathly ill, and you're going to stop it tonight, Mr. Mayor."

Being frightened for his life wasn't enough to scare the politician out of the mayor. "I'm afraid it's not that simple. There needs to be an investigation. We have to see what's being done and give them ninety days to fix the problem…"

"Our children will be dead in a week, so you'll understand why a delay of three months will not work for us. So either fix it now…"

The mayor squirmed to move his head away from the shark woman's approaching jaws, but she was too strong for him to get far.

"Or?"

The shark woman opened her maw wide enough to bite the top third of the Mayor's body off.

Luckily, that's when I caught up to them from the red carpet opening I had been attending. I leapt in the air and landed a flying big shoe kick the Ninja Clown Monks of Newark taught me, right onto the shark woman's nose. Sadly, I was wearing regular shoes or it might have knocked her out instead of just down.

The sharp pain loosened her grip on the Mayor. I pulled him free and tossed him back into the half-open car. His driver, an NYPD officer, stepped out of the car and pointed his gun at the shark woman.

It was a brave but very bad idea.

"Officer, don't shoot her."

"Back off, Bikini Jones. I'm a cop, not some namby-pamby bleeding heart do-gooder in a swimsuit. That animal tried to eat the mayor, so I'm going to end its life."

I placed myself between the shark woman and the officer. My foot hit her hard, but this was a ten-foot-tall, half-ton shark woman. She'd be back on her feet in seconds.

"Officer, your 9mm isn't going to do much except make her bleed. Think about what blood in the air would do to a shark person."

The cop's brow furrowed. "The same as it would to a shark in the water?"

"Exactly, only worse because your shot is going to hurt her, which means the thinking part of her brain is going to give way to the primitive part. She's going to go into a feeding frenzy and there will be nothing left of the three of us. Please get back in the car and drive the Mayor out of here. I'll take care of Matoka. And give me these."

I plucked his TASER, collapsible baton, and pepper spray off his belt then shoved the cop in the driver's seat an instant before the shark's jaws closed on where we'd been standing.

Matoka still got the door—it looked like it had been smashed in by a truck.

Luckily, I had the sense to push myself back when I pushed the cop in.

Seeing the ten-foot shark woman glaring at him through the driver's window, the cop chauffeur put the pedal to the metal, and the limo was doing ninety within seconds.

"Matoka, stop this. The mayor has too much red tape holding him back. Instead of attacking him, you should be working on getting the shark children medical help."

The shark sneered, allowing me the chance to appreciate a truly frightening amount of razor-sharp teeth up close and personal. "Right, because we can just show up at Bellevue and ask for help. It's not like we have human health insurance. Besides, we are sharks transformed into humanoids, not the other way around. Human doctors wouldn't know how to help us."

Matoka and I began circling each other, but I couldn't focus all my attention on the shark woman because I didn't know if she'd come alone. If another of the Mano shark people came at me from behind, I'd end up as sushi.

"What about the Maritime College?" The State University of New York had a campus on the water offshore from the Bronx. "They have Marine biologists."

The shark woman snorted, then followed that with a harsh chuckle that held more sadness than most sobs. "I'm not an idiot, Bikini Jones! I was there earlier today to ask for their help. Do you know what they did? Took one look at me and ran away!"

"Not to be critical, but did you speak to them in a quiet voice or scream your demands at them? At ten feet tall and a thousand pounds, you're bound to be more than a little intimidating to the average human. If you acted angrily, can you blame them for being scared?"

Matoka leaned forward. "Humans are the ones killing Mano babies! They don't have the right to be scared of those they're trying to murder! I thought that maybe you might be the one reasonable human, but you just made it clear where you stand."

Before I could counter, the shark woman leapt with such speed and grace that she looked like she was swimming through the air toward my face, her jaws leading the way. I barely got the baton up in front of me in time to wedge her jaws apart. It was maybe twenty-seven inches long and my hand was holding it wedged in her mouth, which was far too close to her teeth for comfort.

If I didn't come up with a way out of this soon, I was going to end up as chum.

While I figure this out, you might as well see how it all began— at the red carpet opening of a themed restaurant.

2

I'm not a fan of red carpets. Never have been, ever since one came to life and tried to eat me. It was back in the days when I was broke. I'd been fighting an Aztec goddess named Chantico who specialized in heath fires, volcanos, and personal treasures. It was the personal treasure aspect that allowed her to possess anything that someone considered a treasure. Chantico ran amuck, possessing a ridiculous number of inanimate objects. While I tried to stop her from killing people, some film students shadowed me and recorded the whole thing. They made a movie from the footage, including her settling off a volcano on a mini-golf course.

I thought I'd banished her, but she found a workaround so she could even the score at the premier. I've been known to complain about wearing stiletto heels, but that day they were all that stood between me and suffocation.

I had high hopes that this particular red carpet walk would be much less eventful. There were no angry divinities or spirits out to get me who were at large, at least as far as I knew. Plus, this was a restaurant opening by some former adversaries of mine who were trying out life on the straight and narrow. Nothing supernatural involved.

I'd been cajoled into helping three truly old school gangsters make a living without robbing banks and ended up as one of the investors in The Tommy Gunners' Bar and Thrill.

I was lukewarm on the name but was fully behind the idea. Manhattan was a great place for theme restaurants, like the one where you can travel to another planet to eat or where robot ninjas serve your meals. The Bar and Thrill used a prohibition-era speakeasy theme.

"Ain't she a beaut?" The so-called beaut that Joey Capone was referring to wasn't me or Spats Magool, the female member of the Tommy Gunners' trio. And she's found of saying that just because she was a broad–her word, not mine–that didn't mean she has to dress like it. Translation–she dressed in pinstripes and a fedora, same as Joey and Big Lug, although her shoes had the spats from which she got her nickname. She was the only one of the three with a moll, but hers was a guy named Antonio. He wore men's clothes, which were much more colorful than the other three. He wasn't a member of the gang, more along the lines of an intern.

The beaut to which Joey Capone was referring was a 1929 Cadillac in mint condition.

"It certainly is an amazing car," I said.

"Gramps would be touched that we drove to the premier in his car." The Gramps he was referring to was Al Capone. This had been the mobster's car, complete with gun slots, compartments to drop tacks to give flat tires to cops chasing them, and an oil burner that left a smokescreen to throw off pursuers.

Al Capone wasn't biologically Joey's grandfather. Joey had been a history professor specializing in the early 20th century and while exploring Al Capone's vault, hit his head and woke up believing he was the reincarnation of Al Capone's grandson. To this day, I'm not sure why that would be a big deal, but it was for Joey. He formed the Tommy Gunners and went on several crime sprees using modified prohibition-era weapons.

"We're here," Big Lug cooed from the front seat from the driver's seat. "We've got ourselves a big crowd."

Big Lug had a tendency to view the world through cracked rose-colored glasses, so his idea of a crowd might be smaller than most people's. I hadn't been expecting too many folks, but to my surprise, there were easily a hundred people waiting outside, a third of which looked to be reporters or paparazzi.

That was surprising. I figured we'd get a few lookie-loos and maybe a couple of local reporters looking for a human-interest story for the 10 o'clock news, and then only because the Mayor and I were attending.

Of the two of us, I was probably the bigger draw.

I'm not trying to brag. I've become a bit of a celebrity over the years. I guess people like to follow the adventures of a woman in a bikini who saves the world on occasion.

The paparazzi were expected because they knew they'd get a good shot of me. Typically, I wear jewelry that emits ultraviolet light mixed with a few other tricks so cameras can't get a clear shot of my face or any other bits that might help sell a newspaper, magazine, or be used as clickbait. But because I was here to help promote the restaurant, it didn't make much sense for me to not allow photos. I wanted the place to get coverage, which meant I had to do without those gadgets and allow my picture to be taken and circulated, whether I was thrilled with the idea or not. I'd been dieting for a week.

I sported as classy a bikini as I could muster. It was a sporty number that resembled a pinstriped suit. It even had a bow tie where the two top cups met.

I topped the ensemble off with a fedora that was a thank you gift from the Tommy Gunners for my help getting the restaurant open. Thankfully, I could accessorize below my elbows and my knees or above my neck without the clothes disappearing. I wasn't so lucky with clothes put on any other spots.

Stupid curse.

In addition to the headgear, I wore long satin gloves that matched the suit and a pair of sensible high heels that were designed for me to be able to run or fight in.

You'd be surprised how often there's a need for that sort of thing around me.

"This is it, youse guys. Everything we've worked for. Not only did we build the greatest restaurant in Manhattan—" Joey Capone had been what some might consider a supervillain, so he was used to exaggerating. Not that it wasn't a first-class joint with superb chefs, but the best in Manhattan was pushing it a bit. "—but a way of showing this modern generation the glory of the era that holds all our hearts, both in the restaurant and the attached museum."

Joey had spent most of his ill-gotten gains on prohibition mobster paraphernalia collectibles and probably had the most impressive collection of its kind in the world.

"From here on out, it's going to be constant work for all of us, day and night, to make this place a success. So tonight, we take the time to enjoy ourselves before we buckle down. Let's go say hi to our adoring public."

Big Lug grinned. "Go get them, boss."

3

One of the busboys opened the car door and Joey stepped out onto the red carpet and was greeted by camera flashes. Spats Magool exited next, holding a violin case to her side. Yes, there really was an old-fashioned Tommy gun in there, even if the ammo was rubber. The Tommy Gunners were old-school villains, the ones who like the challenge and the money but not so much the death and destruction. Third out was Big Lug from behind the driver's seat. The shocks rose in relief now that it didn't have to support the big man's bulk.

Antonio slid behind the wheel as the hulking man lifted his massive arm and waved to the crowd, then joined the others on the red carpet. Joey Capone looked back towards the open passenger window.

"Antonio, you be careful driving that. It's on loan and it's worth your life if you so much as scratch the paint. And that's selling it cheap."

Joey talked tough, but they weren't killers. Although if anything did happen to the car, I might have to intervene to keep Joey from beating Antonio so badly that he ended up in the hospital.

Reporters yelled questions.

"Mr. Capone, how does it feel to finally be going straight?"

Joey grabbed the lapel of his jacket and tugged on it. "I gotta tell you, it feels real good."

"Do you think you in the Tommy Gunners will be able to stay on the straight and narrow?"

Joey Capone glared. In his mind, the reporter was doubting Joey's word about his intentions to stop being a criminal. The gang leader was about to open his mouth and say something unfortunate when Big Lug stepped in front of him and answered instead.

"Of course. Now that we've got a chance, we'll make the most of it."

Lug was doing great. I noticed someone crouched down on the street side of the car. I leaned over and looked out the Caddy's window. There was what looked to be a teenage boy in a hoodie squatting down.

I wasn't too surprised. I had more than a few fans who were teenage boys. Understandable when you figure that I run around fighting bad guys in a bikini. I turned a handle around in circles to open the window.

"Can I help you?" He probably wanted an autograph or to take a selfie with me. It wouldn't be the first time.

"Bikini Jones, you're the only one who can help me," he whispered in a raspy voice.

I was getting the distinct impression that he was looking for more than a post on social media. His hood covered his face, hiding his features in shadow. And even though it was a warm fall night, he wore gloves.

"Please tell me more," I said as a reporter shouted another question at the Tommy Gunners so loud I turned my head.

"Spats, how do we know this isn't some sort of plan for the Tommy Gunners to hit the Federal Reserve in Manhattan like you did with Fort Knox?"

The lady mobster grinned and pointed the violin case towards the reporter playfully, but from my spot inside the car, I could see Joey's expression as his eyebrows raised and his mouth opened as if he were thinking that was a good idea. Big Lug noticed, then elbowed him gently to bring his boss back to the here and now.

Spats answered. "Because if we were going to do that, we wouldn't have needed to bring in a partner to help us out with the money situation." Spats motioned with her free hand towards the Cadillac. "Ladies and gentlemen, may I present our business partner, the one and only Bikini Jones."

I turned back toward the street and my visitor in the hoodie was gone.

"Antonio, did you see where the kid on the side of the car went?"

The male moll shrugged from the driver's seat. "Sorry, Ms. Jones. I didn't see nobody but I think Spatsy just gave you your cue."

I let him go. It's not unheard of for someone to make up a story in an attempt to send me on a wild goose chase or set a trap. If it was important enough, the kid in the hoodie would come back around. I couldn't waste time chasing everyone who gave me a cryptic message. I wouldn't have time to get anything else done.

I stepped carefully out of the car. There's an art to it for women. Men don't have to worry about a photographer getting a shot of bits you don't want plastered across all media.

Because of my celebrity, sometimes I get greeted with applause or cheers. It was a tad embarrassing but came with the territory, so a shouting crowd didn't faze me.

The surprise didn't show up until a few seconds later when I heard what they were shouting.

"Hell no, she shouldn't show!"

And they kept chanting it over and over.

They held signs that read things like:

Decency, yes! Bikini no!

Ban Bikini Jones!

Harlot be gone!

For a moment, I stood frozen like a deer in headlights. I had instincts and reflexes to rely on if aliens dropped out of the sky and started shooting up things with plasma rifles, but I wasn't quite sure how to deal with people upset by my attire. Sure, over the years I've had to endure people who looked down on me because of how I *had* to dress—yes, for me, wearing a bikini is not a choice. I wish it were. It's an honest-to-goodness magical curse.

But the idea that enough people were upset by it that they banded together to organize a protest messed with my head. I know a lot of people wouldn't believe this, but there are times when I look at my life and feel like I don't deserve my recognition. Or that I don't have the skills the people expected me to have. That the only reason I beat bad guys and monsters was luck and because some mean old witch once got upset at me because her husband was peeping at me while I sunbathed.

I knew in my head that I worked hard to not only get where I am but to be able to do what I do. That doesn't stop imposter syndrome from giving me a twinge of self-doubt every so often.

Thanks to these protesters, it was quickly expanding, but I've learned along the way that there are times you can avoid conflict and times you can't. These protesters already had manufactured a conflict, so I had best figure out what their problems were.

"What seems to be the issue here?" I asked.

A woman in a blonde fusspot haircut tossed her head back and rolled her eyes as if I had asked the single stupidest question that had ever been heard in Manhattan.

"The problem is you!"

"How is it me exactly? The way I saved the world last month? You're not fond of breathing, I take it? Perhaps it's I don't do enough charity work? Tens of thousands of people this month alone now have filters that give them clean and safe drinking water. That isn't enough for you? Obviously, you must've done more, so please tell us all about it?"

The Kvetcher didn't miss a beat. "Don't try to make this about me, Miss Bikini Jones. Although I think people should call you Harlot Jones."

My real name is Mary Sue, but Bikini long ago stuck as a nickname for obvious reasons.

"My love life is none of your concern and one woman trying to slut shame another really sets back the whole sisterhood, don't you think?"

"I'm sure your sex life is just as deviant as you are, but this doesn't even have anything to do with that. It is how you go around dressed, tempting men to look at you."

"In my experience, there are certain types of men who go out looking for temptation." The decent ones at least pretend not to stare. "My having to wear a bikini is something I have no control over."

"A likely story, made up by you to justify your hoochie ways."

"I have to admit, I'm impressed. I haven't heard anyone use hoochie in a sentence in years, so kudos to you for bringing back a classic word used to denigrate women. I'd thank you for taking the time to bring your concerns and insecurities to my attention if there was even one iota of caring in it. You have my personal guarantee that I will do my best to ignore you from here on out."

That set the blonde off. She shouted louder, using language that would make an Atlantean dock worker blush in shame. Not satisfied, she went on to not only question if my parents were married, but if perhaps they were demonic.

I turned, planning to ignore them, but then Big Lug stepped between me and the protesters like a huge human shield.

"You're being very mean to Bikini, so stop it. She's a wonderful person who does nothing but try to make the world a better place and help people. It's not her fault that her wardrobe is so limited."

"Yes it is!" the blonde screamed as spittle flew from her lips into the air. "Only a harlot would dress that way!"

I've been in more than a dozen physical fights and altercations with Big Lug over the years. Despite him being bigger than most gorillas, I've almost always won, and he's never gotten more than mildly miffed. Now his face was red with anger.

That worried me. One, Big Lug didn't always realize his own brute strength. Two, he was well on the way to leading a reformed life. The paparazzi filming him slapping around a woman half his size was not going to help matters.

To my relief, if not confusion, he didn't try to hurt the blonde. Instead, he slipped off his jacket and threw it on the ground, then followed that by taking off his trousers. His fedora never moved from his head.

"Big Lug, what are you…"

The massive mobster waved a hand at me. "Don't worry, Bikini. I gots this." Big Lug was wearing boxers and he pulled the legs up high and then tore the sleeves off his dress shirt. This was followed by him throwing his necktie on the pile along with his jacket and pants. Next, he unbuttoned the top three buttons of his shirt and pulled the bottom up into his man cleavage in a caricature of an old-fashioned country girl outfit.

"If Bikini Jones is a harlot, then I'm one too. What do you think of that, mean lady?"

We never found out because all the blonde could do was sputter. I will admit that he was quite a sight in his homemade bikini, still wearing his leather shoes and black socks that were held up with old school garters.

Big Lug walked over to me and held an elbow out.

"Shall we harlots go in?"

I smiled and took his arm. "We shall."

We walked the rest of the red carpet to the door of the restaurant with Joey falling behind, shaking his head, and waving his hands as if he was speaking. All that came out was, "Why would he do that?"

Spats patted Joey on the back. "That's just Lug."

"But we're going to look like fools on the news," Joey whispered.

Spats shook her head. "I don't think so. Remember, we're on the same side as Bikini Jones this time. The media love her, so maybe they'll be kind to us."

4

When we reached the door, I knocked. A wooden slat slid to the side, revealing a rectangular hole in the door with our maître d' Simon staring out at us.

"Password?"

"Swordfish."

That was part of the gimmick. You had to make reservations, although you could do that from right outside the restaurant as the number was posted there. With your reservation, you got a password which is the only way to get into the restaurant.

The maître d' opened the door and we all walked in. The Mayor, a couple of City Council people, and a handful of Broadway actors were already there and seated. They were all wearing matching fedoras, gifts for the A-listers, in hopes they would post about the place on social media.

Big Lug's new look was getting a lot of stairs. Normally, Big Lug is the type that gets embarrassed easily, but there was still enough fire in his eyes that I don't think he honestly cared. I stood up on my toes and kissed him on the cheek. "Thanks, big guy."

Lug's entire face went beet red. "It weren't nothing, Bikini. If it wasn't for you, we'd all probably be back in jail by now. Now we got real jobs, a place to live, and I finally got a dog."

"Bootlegger is a very good dog and you've taken wonderful care of her."

"Thanks, Bikini. I converted the end of the hallway back there into a little doggie house so I can check on her while I'm working or take her out for a walk if she needs it."

Big Lugs saw Joey Capone giving him a come hither shake of his head.

"Sorry Bikini, I've got to get to work. I hope you enjoy your meal and the show."

Joey Capone looked like he was shouting but managed to keep his voice to a whisper as he went up one side of Big Lug and down the other, all the while pointing towards his boxers and bikini style shirt. Big Lug crossed his arms over his massive chest and shook his head. Exasperated, Joey put his hands together like he was pleading just as Antonio came in, having picked up Big Lug's clothes from the red carpet. Big Lug uncrossed his arms and nodded. It looked like they had reached a compromise. Big Lug kept his homemade bikini but put his pinstriped jacket and tie back on.

Motion from the corner of the room caught my eye. A young girl and a dog were waving their hand and paw respectively at me. I waved back.

The dog wasn't the one Big Lug had adopted. This one had the brain of the mad scientist, Dr. Dendrite. The girl was Harper, Dendrite's daughter although she didn't know it. Dr. D was a silent investor in the restaurant. As much as I would've liked to have sat with Harper, Joey had me seated at the same table with the Mayor.

I joined my tablemates. His honor extended his hand and I shook it.

"Hello, Mr. Mayor."

"Hello, Bikini. A pleasure to see you, especially when the city's not in danger." The mayor paused for a second and crinkled his brow, looked at me, and then back over at the Tommy Gunners. "The city's not in danger, is it?"

I chuckled. "Not as far as I know."

That got a smile from the Mayor and everyone else at the table.

"That's good enough for me."

I'd barely sat down when Joey Capone reached under his jacket, pulled out a gun, and fired once at the ceiling.

Blanks.

"Now that I have all youse attention, let me welcome you to the opening night of the Tommy Gunners' Bar and Thrill. Speaking on behalf of me and the gang, I'm real happy all youse VIPs decided to join us here tonight. You're in for a heck of a good time and a fantastic meal, so without any further ado, let the festivities begin."

5

The dining experience started out well. As we ate our salads, the Tommy Gunners, along with the waitstaff, explained how the evil Mayor was out to get them, a bit of good-natured humor directed at His Honor. A couple of the restaurant bloggers were filming the whole thing, so the mayor laughed good-naturedly. Then we heard about a rival gang that they were hoping wouldn't attack as loaves of bread were brought out, followed by enough pasta to choke a horse which is when the steel front door had its hinges cut through by a glowing beam from the outside and fell flat on the floor. A man dressed as a cowboy, including a neckerchief tied around his face, rode a robotic horse through the door. I doubted it wanted any pasta.

I rolled my eyes.

Electro-Bo.

He was another villain with a theme. While the Tommy Gunners went for retro prohibition gangsters, Bo went for steampunk cowboy. His gimmick was electricity-based gadgets like an electricity slinging six-gun and a lariat style lasso that packed enough of a wallop to knock out a rhino.

His first crime spree had been to steal the parts he needed to build Old Zap. That's what he named his horse. When he was caught, all the purloined high-tech went back to its original owners, but they couldn't take the brain as Bo had not only created but programmed it to behave as a very intelligent horse would.

Most people assume that most of these so-called supervillains aren't that smart, at least when it comes to common sense, as they always seem to get caught. And there's a certain amount of truth to that, but I would use the term shortsighted over dumb. After all, someone who built a robot brain and electricity discharging gadgets isn't dumb by any means. It turns out that Bo wasn't shortsighted either. As he was putting together his robot horse for the first time, he took the time to make a 3D scan of each piece he used, including his modifications.

When Bo broke out of jail, he stole three industrial-grade 3D printers, a ton of ABS plastic and carbon fiber, and made himself a new Old Zap.

As he was careful to program Old Zap to never hurt anyone fatally, he got the mechanical horse back upon his latest release from prison.

He had assured his parole board he was going straight. Looks like he may have lied on that point.

"A fine evening to y'all. I can tell just by looking, that all you fine folks are very intelligent people, so y'all realize this here is a stickup. If y'all cooperate, there won't be any problems and no one'll get hurt. I'm just here for your valuables and cash." The horse spit out an old-fashioned canvas sack and held it with its teeth. Old Zap placed it in front of the nearest diner.

"Kindly take the sack and place your jewelry and other valuables inside of it, along with any cash you might have secreted on your person. Then pass it along to the next person who should do the same and so on, until everyone has been properly robbed."

Joey Capone stomped to within five feet of the horse and started yelling and sputtering at the same time while looking up at the mounted cowboy. "Bo, what in the name of my gangster grandpa do you think you're doing?"

Bo nodded towards Joey. "I thought that'd be obvious, Capone. I'm robbing your joint."

Joey squinted and looked genuinely confused. "Why? I thought we was friends?"

Bo frowned. "I thought we was too, then you no good sidewinders did me wrong. I'm just here to even the score."

Bo pointed his six-shooter the Joey Capone's chest and pulled the trigger. Instead of a boom, there was a zap, and Joey was hit in the chest with one of the villainous cowboy's electro-bullets which knocked him to the ground.

Spats reached for her violin case, pulled out her Tommy gun, and opened fire. The impact of the rubber bullets knocked Electro-Bo off Old Zap but otherwise didn't do the cowboy villain much harm, except knock his ten-gallon hat off his head. He was wearing 3D-printed body armor underneath his red shirt.

Big Lug lifted Joey Capone like he was a rag doll and put him behind the bar while Electro-Bo put his hat back on while he tried to get Spats in his sites, but she threw over a table and ducked behind it as the two began exchanging their own unique brands of gunfire.

All the VIPs dropped down to hide behind their tables. The Mayor, having been subjected to villainous attacks on a semi-regular basis, did them one better and flattened himself against the floor. I got up from the table and noticed Dr. Dendrite's dog collar suddenly sported a robot arm with a rather nasty-looking ray gun held in it. He'd turned the over a new leaf and was living a better life as a dog than he had as a human, but he might do something stupid to protect his daughter Harper.

I caught his eye and shook my head. The small dog's lips curled up in what might've been the start of a snarl, but he nodded. The robot arm disappeared back into his collar.

I grabbed a large plastic tray and held it in front of me as I snuck up behind the steampunk cowboy.

Bo turned his head and saw me. The cowboy greeted me with a tip of his ten-gallon hat and a smile. "Good evening, Bikini Jones. I heard you might be here, so I made sure to plan for the occasion. Get her, Old Zap."

As Bo dove back behind the maître d' stand, the robotic horse reared up, just barely keeping from hitting the ceiling with his head.

I was going to need more than a plastic tray. Blue electric bolts shot out of the horse's eyes and hit exactly where I had been standing, but I wasn't there anymore. I was down and rolling to my left, but the horse had planned on that. Old Zap opened its mouth, shooting a blob at me. Instead of a glob of mucus or the equine equivalent of a hairball, the projectile expanded and a second later I was snared in a metal net that shocked me.

It hurt, but not as bad as it should have as my long gloves were lined with Kevlar—a nonconductor—and my high heels were made from a non-conductive resin.

My entire non-bikini wardrobe is designed for function, fighting, and fashion.

I struggled to stand with my gloved arms holding the net to the side to minimize how much touched my bare skin.

The key to getting out of this mess was ditching the net before the horse trampled me flat. I maneuvered over to the coatroom and threw myself over the counter, catching the top of the net on a hat hook. As I went down, the net stayed up and I squirmed my way free, although the jolts it was putting out knocked out the coatroom lights.

The robot horse came at me over the counter, hooves first. I grabbed one and used its momentum to pull it in faster. The equine robot plummeted forward, its limbs splayed out in different directions.

The coatroom had a gag shelf customers could see, filled with things gangsters might've checked-guns, brass knuckles, a hand grenade, and an old-fashioned crowbar.

Crowbar in hand, I sat on the robot's back and rammed it into the horse's right rear hip, then pulled hard. The plastic bowl holding the hip joint in place cracked. I repositioned the crowbar and repeated the maneuver until the leg fell off and then repeated it on the right front leg. The robotic horse was programmed to walk like a real one with movement at the opposite front and rear legs on either side. By getting rid of the limbs, I effectively limited it to moving in awkward circles. I dropped the crowbar. An iron weapon wasn't a great idea against a bad guy who shot electricity. Instead, I picked up the horse's front leg and climbed back over the coatroom counter.

Spats and Antonio were writhing on the ground. They must have taken an electro-bullet. Big Lug put himself between them and Bo.

The steampunk cowboy emptied the rest of his six-shooters at Lug. It must have been causing him agony, but the bug guy acted as if the shots annoyed him about as much as a bee sting and he kept his feet.

Bo holstered his guns and pulled out his lariat, then lassoed the big man. The zap from the rope was bright enough to throw shadows all over the room and I could swear I smelled flesh sizzling.

Big Lug dropped to his knees moaning.

I lunged at Bo, swinging his horse's plastic leg like a club, when another rope wrapped itself around my arms and chest. I braced myself but still got yanked backward.

I had underestimated the robot horse. Just because he was stuck in the coatroom didn't mean Old Zap was helpless. His remaining front leg was also a grappling hook launcher which had me hooked like a prize trout.

Grinning, Electro-Bo stood over me, pointing one of his six-guns. I struggled to free myself as he reloaded.

Big Lug was still conscious and saw what was happening. He pushed against the lasso that bound his arms to his sides.

As if in answer to the big man's yells, there was a yappy bark from the back of the restaurant. I turned, half expecting Dr. Dendrite to be trying to help, but the sound didn't come from the dog with the brain of a mad scientist. It was Bootlegger, Big Lug's dog.

You'd think someone Lug's size would have chosen a mastiff or Irish wolfhound or some other huge breed, but he didn't. Instead, he went to the pound and picked the runt of the place. Bootlegger was maybe twenty inches long, nose to tail. Even with short legs, the mutt made good time crossing the restaurant and took up a position in front of her master, growling and barking at the villainous cowboy.

Bo jumped back as if he was startled. "Is that a sewer rat with a collar?" he said, pointing his gun at the dog.

A bellow of rage and pain shook all the furniture in the room and made everyone, including Bo, freeze. Big Lug snapped the electric lariat and charged Bo faster than I'd ever seen the big guy move.

A second later, Lug lifted Bo with one of his huge mitts around the cowboy's throat. The other bent Bo's wrist back far enough that he dropped his six-gun.

"Don't you dare hurt Miss Bootlegger!"

"That's your dog?" Bo squeaked. Even as angry as he was, Lug hadn't cut off the cowboy's airway. "I would never hurt an animal, especially a dog."

I'd managed to unwind myself from the horse's grappling line and wrapped it around a chair, so when I let go the chair popped back and smashed into Old Zap, knocking the robot back inside the coatroom.

I ran over to the big guy and placed a gentle hand on his shoulder. "It's okay, Lug. Bo won't hurt Miss Bootlegger. You can put him down."

Lug didn't move. His eyes never left the cowboy's now very red face. "Bikini, he was going to hurt *my* dog. Nobody hurts my dog."

"It was a misunderstanding. I think your dog just scared him. I don't think Bo would've hurt Miss Bootlegger."

"I wouldn't. You know me, Lug," squeaked the cowboy. "I love animals."

"Miss Bootlegger is fine. You can put Bo down."

I watched as Big Lug's eyes and mouth twitched. He then turned to see his dog sitting and looking up at him, wagging her tail.

"Are you okay, Miss Bootlegger?"

The dog wagged her tail faster.

"You're a good dog."

"Definitely a good dog," rasped Bo.

Lug turned back, then slowly lowered his arm to return Bo to the floor. I quickly took off the cowboy's gun belt and removed his other weapons.

"Lug, I'm sorry about your dog," Bo said, rubbing his throat. "Honest, I wouldn't hurt have hurt her once I realized she was a dog."

Big Lug bent down and stretched out his arms. The tiny dog leapt into them. Lug hugged Miss Bootlegger. She licked his face and he was instantly back to his normal lovable self.

The rest of the gang was back on their feet.

"Why would you do this to us?" Joey screamed.

"Did you know how important this night is?" Spats spat.

"If it's so important, why didn't you invite me?" Bo said, sticking out his bottom lip and crossing his arms over his chest.

"We did invite you, ya dumb mook. But not for tonight. Tonight is for the bigwigs and the VIPs. You're invited tomorrow night when we open up for a special night for our pals."

"I didn't get an invitation."

Joey Capone turned to look at Lug, who was petting Miss Bootlegger and making funny faces at her. He stopped long enough to answer, "I sent an email."

"I'm telling you, I didn't get it."

Spats rolled her eyes, glared at Bo, and tapped her toes. "Did you check your spam filter?"

Bo pulled out his cell phone and I looked around the room. The people who had been hiding behind the tables were now climbing back into their seats. The bloggers were all still filming. If this hit the papers as a robbery by one of their old former villain friends, folks would be too afraid to eat there. The Tommy Gunners' Grill and Thrill would be out of business within the month.

I wasn't about to let that happen so I spoke into my digital wristwatch. It's a bit more advanced than the latest commercially available model, although a typical smartwatch could have accomplished this task too.

My words were turned into a text which was then sent to Dr. Dendrite. I heard his dog collar ping. A second later a holographic display floated in front of him. He read the message looked at me and nodded, then whispered to Harper. A second later she got her feet and started clapping as Bo turned red as he realized he had indeed been invited.

Other people picked up the clapping, hesitantly at first and then louder. It didn't suddenly become a standing ovation, but it was legitimate applause, mainly because the canvas sack hadn't been passed, yet so no one technically had been robbed.

The once time villains stopped and turned to look at the diners, confused

Joey Capone stepped close to me and whispered, "What the heck's going on, Bikini? Why are the mooks applauding?"

"At your bit of dinner theater," I said with a whisper and a wink. Louder, I added, "Everyone line up and take a bow."

I didn't have to tell Big Lug twice. He took his bow then held Miss Bootlegger, so that she took a bow, then lifted her paw to wave at the crowd. Spats, Joey, I, and a very confused Bo all bowed as well.

"I hope you enjoyed the special treat we set up for opening night. Sit back and relax. Your entrées will be out momentarily." I motioned the Tommy Gunners and Bo towards the kitchen.

"So are we out of business?" Joey said.

I shook my head. "Not yet. All your VIPs think that was all part of the show."

Spats Magool peeked out the window to look at the crowd. "And they liked it?"

I shrugged. "They didn't hate it. In fact, if we spin it the right way, it might actually boost business."

Spats turned and squinted in my direction. "How do you figure that, Bikini?"

"People are always fascinated with villains. They tune in to the news and internet to watch the latest heist on TV from a safe distance. You guys could treat this like long-running Broadway shows that bring in famous people to play lead parts."

Joey's eyes lit up. "So that people go to shows who wouldn't normally go because they want to see the star in person. So those mooks are going to come here to see famous villains."

"Exactly. You could hire a special guest villain every month or two and have them pretend to rob the place each night. People would pay to experience that safely in person," I said.

Spats smiled and gently pushed her fist into her other open palm. "And we get to help other villains go straight. No one ever wants to hire us which is part of why we always go back to crime."

"That and the attention," Antonio said.

"And this way we get both," Joey said.

"That's a great idea. Don't you think so, Miss Bootlegger?" Big Lug asked the dog and waited for an answer. He didn't get a nod or shake of the head but he got licked again on his cheek which made him smile.

"Does that mean you guys are hiring me for this month?" Electro-Boh said.

"You robbed us for real. You're lucky I don't turn you over to the cops myself," Joey grumbled.

Bo's head bowed and he took off his ten-gallon hat to place it over his chest. "I'm frightfully sorry about what I done. I was just steamed cause I thought we was friends and that you guys didn't care enough to invite me."

"And you shot me with them stinking electro bullets. Maybe I'll just put you in a pair of cement shoes and let you go swimming in the Hudson."

"Don't be like that, Joey," Bo said.

"Boss, Bikini could have had us arrested last time we committed a crime, but she didn't. She even helped us out opening this place. We can't really pay her back…"

Joey reached up and slapped the back of Lug's head. Miss Bootlegger growled at the gangster boss. "Can't pay her back? She gets twenty percent of the profits. We're gonna be paying her back forever."

Lug shook his head, unphased by the slap. "I meant for being nice to us. She doesn't need us to be nice to her."

"I may not have needed it, but I appreciate your outfit change earlier."

"I was wondering about that. Why is Big Lug in some sort of

gangster bikini thing?"

"I explain it to you later," Spats said.

"But we can be nice to Bo and pay it forward that way. That way he can tell people he has a job and maybe they'll give him another one." Big Lug said.

Bo sighed and put his hat back on his head. "I don't know 'bout that. Most folks ain't so forgiving. I mean, what am I going to do for a living?"

"You made a horse robot with advanced AI. You could adapt that for cars to keep people safe. You could modify some of your weapons to provide nonlethal options for law enforcement and the military. You do that the right way and you could be rich."

It always made me wonder why geniuses like Bo returned to crime instead of just marketing their inventions. Not that marketing and promotions are easy by any means, but neither is robbing a bank or an armored car.

"But where am I going to get the money to hire patent lawyers so that I don't get ripped off?" Bo asked.

Big Lug turned to me and smiled. "Bikini helped us out. Maybe she could help you."

Bo looked at me with eyes bigger and sadder than Miss Bootlegger could have managed.

Looks like I was going to help another villain go legit. "I have lawyers on staff. We could try to mass-produce your inventions under Bikini Enterprises, but I run a business, not a charity." Actually, I do both. My charity is the Bikini Foundation which is in large part funded by Bikini Enterprises. "My team is going to be doing most of the work to bring it to market so we would take the lion's share of the profits for the first couple years until we make our money back."

Bo sighed and looked at the floor. "And probably the patents too."

"No. The patents would be yours." Bo perked up again. "However, for me to invest that kind of time and money, I'm going to want an exclusive contract."

Bo was jumping up and down so much that he looked like he was doing a hoedown. "So you'd do all the work…"

"Only in regard to manufacturing, patenting, and distribution. I expect you to turn up every day for work so you can improve these things so they would work better for the areas we would market them in."

"And I would get paid money without having to steal it?"

I nodded.

"You think it would be enough that I could afford an apartment in Manhattan? Or at least Brooklyn?"

"I would put you on salary as staff at Bikini Enterprises so you'll definitely be able to afford Brooklyn. Manhattan if you're careful. However, if you manage to adapt your robotic brain to work with cars so they could self-drive and protect the passengers and react in real-time via your AI, you will be able to buy your own apartment building in Manhattan. Maybe an entire block of them. You might be a billionaire. And if we can provide law enforcement with non-lethal weapons, you'll be even richer. But this won't happen overnight. I won't let something go out unless it's been tested to the point where I'm sure nothing's going to go wrong. It'll probably take years."

"Can I bring Old Zap to work with me?"

A robotic horse wouldn't be the oddest being that shows up for work in Bikini Tower.

"Sure. Although you'll have to reattach two legs I broke off."

"No problem. I pre-printed off some extra joints. It will only take me a couple of hours to fix. When could I start?"

"It will take a bit for my lawyers to draw up a contract. Then I recommend that you hire lawyers to look it over make and sure you're happy with it before you sign. I'd say probably sometime in the middle of next month."

Bo stomped his foot as he swung his arm in front of himself and slapped his thigh. "That's perfect. That means I can work here for a month first."

"Wait a second. I never said you could work here," Joey said.

"I say we hire Bo," Big Lug said.

"Well, this ain't a democracy. I'm the boss. You don't get a say," Joey Capone said.

"Sorry boss, but that ain't true at the Bar and Thrill. In the gang, you is and always will be the boss," Spats said. "However in the restaurant, you, me, and Lug all own equal shares with Bikini and Dr. D owning the rest. We all get a say. Bo gave me a good tussle. The problem with going straight is you can go rusty in the skills department. I vote we hire him for the month. And then we recruit more of our pals tomorrow night when they come to the party."

Big Lug raised his hand in the air. "I vote we hire Bo." Then he lifted his dog's paw. "Miss Bootlegger votes to hire him too."

"Miss Bootlegger doesn't get a vote, you mook," Joey grumbled.

"She gets half of mine," Lug said.

Spats turned to me. "What about you, Bikini?"

I looked at Bo. "You give me your word as a cowboy that you are going to work hard, do this job right, and play it straight?"

Bo took off his hat and placed it over his heart. "I do so solemnly swear."

To be honest, I had no idea what his word as a cowboy was worth, so I added, "Also remember that if you don't do well here, I probably won't give you the other job, comprende?"

"As clear as the finest crystal, ma'am. I will do the best job of pretending to rob this place that you've ever seen."

"I guess one of us better go out and get Dr. Dendrite to find out what his vote is," Spats said.

In answer, beams of light came out of a knob on the ceiling and formed a hologram of Dr. Dendrite's doggy head. "No need Spats. I say give Bo a chance."

Joey's cheeks turned pink. "Dr. D, are you spying on us?"

"Not at all. I told you I would install a state-of-the-art security system. I can monitor everything here from my collar."

"That means you was spying on us!"

"Only in the most literal interpretation."

"Well, don't be listening in unless you tell us you is listening," Joey scolded.

"Very well. I'll be listening."

"You mean all the time?"

"The security system will be recording everything. I'll only listen to the parts I think would be interesting. Now if you excuse me, I'm going to give my full attention back to Harper."

"You mean you were ignoring her to eavesdrop on us?" I said.

The holographic head of doggy Dendrite smirked. "Please. As if a mega genius such as myself can't keep track of three things simultaneously. My brain is chipped into my collar and I can easily listen to her tell me about her upcoming dance recital as the rest of you discuss this business. Carry on."

The light beams blinked off and Dendrite disappeared.

"Wait," Big Lug said. "What was the third thing he was paying attention to?"

I shrugged then we all turned towards Joey Capone.

"I guess the last vote is yours, boss," Spats said.

"C'mon boss, he a good guy," Big Lug said. "If youse do, I'll let Miss Bootlegger lick your face."

"Do youse know where that tongue has been? I've seen that mangy mutt clean herself. Keep it away from me."

Bo held his ten-gallon hat in both hands and looked down at the floor. "So what's it going to be, Joey? I know I screwed up and I'm sorry. Give me the chance to make it up to you."

The man who claimed to be the reincarnated grandson of Al Capone stroked his chin.

I'm sure Joey Capone realized that even if he voted no, those of us who voted yes owned over fifty percent of the restaurant, so technically Bo was already hired, but the last thing the Tommy Gunners needed was a rift between them.

"Fine, youse hired, but I gots a date Monday afternoon and I want you and Old Zap to take us in a carriage ride around Central Park."

The cowboy and the gangster shook. "Deal."

6

The rest of the evening was uneventful, although the protesters stayed outside until after the restaurant was closed.

I made the rounds and said my goodbyes. The Tommy Gunners assured me they had everything under control. My last goodbye was to the mayor.

"I have to say Bikini that the beginning of the show was very convincing. I actually thought we were being robbed."

"All part of the thrill," I said. "From now on they'll be handing out some fake jewelry and such to people when they come in so when the robbery happens they can turn those over instead of their own valuables." It was Big Lug's idea and it was a good one.

"My car's out back." We walked toward the back door. "Can I give you a lift back to Bikini Tower?"

The Mayor was under the common misconception that I lived at the Tower. I had a room there where I stayed when I needed to, but I keep a small apartment of my own. Sometimes it was nice just to get away from it all even if it's just for a few hours.

"No thank you, Mayor. I'm going to walk home."

"It is almost midnight and despite the best efforts of myself and the NYPD, there are still some parts of New York where it's not safe for a woman to walk alone in the middle of the night."

I leaned back, crossed my arms over my chest, and cocked an eyebrow, a look similar to what a first-grade teacher would give a student who told them two plus two was equal to five.

The Mayor had the decency to look embarrassed and his face flushed. "Sorry, Bikini. I guess I wasn't thinking about who I was talking to, now was I? You handle yourself better than a half dozen cops." His driver, a police officer, grimaced unhappily as that. "My apologies for saying something so demeaning and sexist."

I uncrossed my arms and nodded. "Apology accepted."

Although his mention of cops got me thinking that it wouldn't be a bad idea to talk to the Tommy Gunners about running a first responders' night every month and offering New York's Finest,

Bravest, and First on the Scene a discount as a way of saying thanks.

The mayor and I both left by the back, with his driver opening the door for us.

The mayor climbed into his waiting limo. The driver closed his door then got behind the wheel and drove off. The car merged into traffic, which is when I noticed the dark gray dorsal fin maneuvering between other vehicles to follow it.

I started running and you already know what happened when I caught up.

Which brings you, dear reader, up to speed on how I ended up pinned beneath a thousand-pound shark woman with a small baton the only thing standing between me and decapitation, shark style.

I have may have grown up in Newark, New Jersey but there's no place like the Big Apple. In Boise or Ithaca, a woman in a bikini fighting a giant shark person would be enough to stop traffic.

Not in New York.

As I struggled to not lose an arm to Matoka's jaws, nighttime traffic just veered around us as if we were no more out of place than a couple of traffic cones. One cab driver, annoyed at having to change lanes, laid on his horn as he passed which was annoying enough for Matoka to turn her head. The cabby and shark woman flipped each other off.

I'd tucked the Taser and the pepper spray into opposite sides of my bikini bottom. Before she could turn back, I pulled out the pepper spray and aimed it straight at the gills on her neck.

The shock and pain made her lurch away from me as she struggled for breath. Although shark people could breathe air, messing with her gills still affected Matoka's air supply. I scrambled away on all fours, having a little trouble with breathing and tearing eyes myself. Pepper spray is effective but fickle. A light breeze turned some of it back at me.

That didn't stop me from firing the Taser at where her spinal cord met her shark brain. I pulled the trigger once, then twice. The third time the batteries died.

The shark woman was still conscious and even angrier.

My curse makes it difficult for me to carry weapons. There are times I can manifest a bikini with a holster and carry a neural disruptor but armed and dangerous wasn't the look I was aiming for at the Bar and Thrill opening.

My watch holds a cornucopia of tiny weapons. I used a low-grade energy beam to cut open the Taser. The beam wasn't powerful enough to do much damage to a living being which was on purpose. The watch housed three small tranquilizer darts, any of which would've been enough to take down most people this side of Big Lug. I fired all three into the shark woman's dark gray hide.

It made her yawn, but that was long enough for me to pull the power cable out of my watch and hook it to the Taser. The battery in my watch is a space-age wonder and could power a suburban house for decades. Bypassing the trigger controls, the jolt I sent from my watch into the Taser had more than a hundred times the strength of the first three zaps.

Twitching from the artificial lightning made Matoka's body dance and convulse violently. I stopped and, with a Herculean effort, the shark woman rolled onto her stomach to crawl in my direction.

"Matoka, please stop. I want to help your people, not hurt you," I said.

"I'll eat you up and crap you out, Bikini Jones," she whispered.

I believed she'd try, so I adjusted my watch and sent a stronger jolt into her hide. Her convulsions were worse but this time when I turned it off, the shark woman wasn't moving.

Very carefully, I moved in to check her vitals. Thankfully, she was still breathing.

I switched my watch to emergency communication mode to the team working the night shift in my hangar Bikini Tower.

"This is Air Bikini Two. Bikini One, do you require pick up?" asked Aditte, my best pilot, as a hologram of her appeared above my watch.

Aditte was one of the mole people, but she left the world beneath because she wanted to fly. Humans weren't too keen on her being around, let alone giving her flying lessons, so she had it rough. Things got even worse when she attracted the attention of Professor Corruzione, a mad scientist who got his jollies by grafting pieces of mutated animals onto people. Thrilled to have another species of humanoid to experiment on, he grafted mutated bat wings to Aditte.

The mole woman became one of Professor Corruzione's

henchpeople. She helped him rob and steal, but refused to kill for him, even when he threatened to remove her wings. Aditte helped me take him down and lost her wings in the process. She was arrested, but I testified on her behalf and she turned state's evidence against Professor Corruzione and got six months. When she got out, I arranged for her to train for her pilot's license. She was a natural. I ended up hiring her and now she flies the Saturn shuttlecraft that was in the pot during the same poker game in which I won Bikini Tower. Now she practically lived in the hangar in case I needed her.

"Isn't this your night off?" I said.

"Do you need your best pilot or not?"

"Truthfully, any pilot would do," I said, watching the shocked look on the mole woman's face at the teasing. "I need a large containment cube."

At ten feet and a thousand pounds, the shark woman barely qualified as large. You don't want to know the things that need an XXXL.

"It's for a very angry but currently unconscious shark woman so I needed it at my location fast before she becomes conscious."

"I'll be there before you know it. Aditte out."

7

I stood over the unconscious shark woman, holding the souped-up TASER and waving traffic to go around us so Matoka didn't get hit by a car.

Minutes later, Aditte and my shuttlecraft arrived and hovered above us. The tractor beam turned the night blue as it lowered the containment cube. I'd designed the cubes with considerable help from Henrietta Houdini, the greatest escape artist in the solar system. She took over for Darcy Dhodinna, the world's greatest escape artist, when her last escape took a turn for the worse.

The cube was automated and once I identified the prisoner, it rolled over to the shark woman, extended metal manacles to encircle her, and then pulled her inside the cube. Forty-six seconds after the containment cube hit the ground, Matoka was secured inside.

"Ready for liftoff," I said into my watch. An instant later, Aditte turned the tractor beam back on and the containment cube floated up to the bottom bay of the shuttlecraft. When it had about a two-story head start, I jumped into the beam with my arms outstretched and spun myself as I floated up into the sky. It wasn't flying, but it was still fun. And going second assured the cube wouldn't accidentally crush me from behind if I didn't move out of the way quick enough.

A mechanical arm plucked the cube out of the beam and secured it onto the floor of the bay. A second smaller arm gently pulled me out of the beam onto the deck.

A hologram of my pilot appeared in front of me.

"Where to? Rikers Island?" Aditte asked.

I shook my head. "Not yet. Set course for the shark people colony in the East River."

"Not to second-guess you…"

I smirked. "Which you do fairly consistently."

"True enough but aren't there shark people living there?"

"It's not called the mole people colony," I said. "And it wouldn't be much of a colony if they weren't."

"So is it really a good idea for us to be visiting them on their home surf after you've taken one of their own prisoner? Shark people are exceptionally strong, especially in water. *The Brass Ring*—" which is what I named the shuttlecraft after I won it. It was from Saturn and in the old days people tried to reach a brass ring while on the merry-go-round to win a prize and considering what is around that planet, it seemed appropriate. "—is pretty tough but I don't see the point of taking her into danger."

Aditte was a tad protective of the ship. Don't get me wrong. That's a good thing, but at the end of the day, it's my ship.

"Noted."

The holographic mole woman sighed. "Which is what you say when you're about to ignore my extremely wise suggestion."

I nodded. "Matoka attacked the Mayor because shark kids are getting deathly ill. I like to see what we can do to help them."

"So you are saying this trip is not an unnecessary danger, but a necessary one."

"Exactly," I said. "Call Bikini Tower and have them prep the infirmary wing, call in anyone who might be able to help, especially those specializing in xenobiology or marine life. Have them call Dr. Dendrite too." His specialty was brains and nervous systems but in the past, the man has transplanted his brain into everything from his current dog body to a T-Rex and a ridiculous variety in between, including a large, mechanical ape called Chimpazoid. He might have insights more typically thinking doctors could miss. "Also make sure they put our security teams on high alert."

"You're worried about the kids causing a ruckus?"

"No, the parents."

"Why would you bring the parents?"

"They aren't going to want to leave their children and I don't blame them," I said.

"Bikini, this is another one of those suggestions you're probably just going to ignore but I have to point out that letting a large number of full-grown shark people inside Bikini Tower is a very dangerous idea. The shark people ate a bunch of surfers at Rockaway Beach."

"Technically, that was only one shark man, and he was sent to the specialty wing at Rikers Island. The rest of the shark people have promised not to harm humans or pets. And until tonight they've kept their word. I'm willing to give them the benefit of the doubt, especially since they know we'll be trying to help their kids."

"It's your skyscraper. ETA four minutes to the East River. You coming to the bridge?" Aditte said.

I shook my head. "I need to get prepped for my chat with the shark people."

"It would be much safer to do that here on the bridge via hologram."

"Won't work. The shark people would see that as a sign of cowardice and will be less inclined to believe my motives were altruistic."

"Fine but I will have *The Brass Ring's* guns armed."

It wasn't a bad idea. "Keep the power levels adjusted to stop the shark people, not kill them."

Aditte chuckled. "You never let me have any fun."

8

There was a slight bump as we broke the surface of the East River. The ship can go underwater as easily as in space. Those Saturnians do quality work.

Due to one aspect of my curse, when I take off a bikini, a new one appears in seconds to minutes. I've learned to use that to my advantage. By focusing, I can control the material and style of the new bathing suit. I changed into one that was insulated, had a pair of holsters, and an empty utility belt.

My preferred sidearm is a neural disrupter because it's generally non-lethal but it wouldn't work where I was heading. If I fired in the East River, the energy would disperse through the water and zap everything it touched, including me.

Being knocked out around Mano would make me a tempting and helpless snack. Definitely high on my not-to-do list.

Instead, I opted for a pair of guns that use a burst of air to propel projectiles. The one on my right hip fired bullet-sized concussion grenades that exploded on impact but had no shrapnel which allowed my opponent to get back up again, hopefully at a much later time. The one on my left hip held tranquilizer darts, much bigger than the ones in my watch. I adjusted the dosage so one should knock out a shark person in less than thirty seconds. I would've liked to get that time frame down to a few seconds but anything that worked quicker had a higher chance of killing someone.

Last, I donned a pair of gauntlets that went over my forearms. Each shot out a hundred high-velocity needles per second. These could be lethal and I wore them only as a last resort.

I put on a specially designed wetsuit that covered all of me except for my face and had openings that sealed around the holsters. While it's true that I can't wear any clothes over a bikini or they'd disappear, I had found a loophole the first time I had to go into outer space—in a dangerous environment, I can wear clothes if they are transparent as they don't hide the fact that I'm wearing a bikini.

I spent a lot of time and money developing this material. In the air, you'd have to look very hard to tell I was wearing anything at all. Plus, the material can be thickened to double as body armor. The wetsuit could hold up to the bite of a moderately sized Great White, so it would probably protect me from one of the Mano.

Adopting technology I first saw on another planet, I compressed twelve hours of breathable air into a tube just a little larger than a breakfast sausage. It was attached to my scuba mask, which had a holographic display that included sonar and vision enhancers that would let me see through the river water as if it was only a mild fog.

I adjusted the containment cube so that Matoka woke as *The Brass Ring* came to a stop and floated near the shark people colony.

The shark woman's battle roar would have let me know she was awake if the sensors hadn't.

"First you capture me and now you come to kill my people!"

"You sure wake up cranky. Not a morning person, are you? Would you like me to have the cube generate you some coffee?"

"You make light before committing genocide on my people? I knew the others were wrong about you helping us."

Matoka shook her entire body to try to escape, but the cube was too well designed and dampened her kinetic force to next to nothing.

"After what I did to help your people not get slaughtered and find you a place to form your colony, you should have a little more faith in me. I'm here to help the shark children get the care that they need."

"You won't lull me in with your lies, Bikini Jones!"

Shrugging I said, "Let's see if my actions change your mind."

I switched on the view screen in front of her cube and went out the bottom of the ship's bay. The tractor beam was off, but the holding field let me go for a dive and kept the river water out.

My suit had regular flippers and web gloves so I moved at a good clip toward the caverns of the shark people, stopping fifty feet from the cave mouth. I wasn't foolhardy enough to go into the dark opening. The shark people might think I'm invading their home.

Using my tongue, I switched my mask's bullhorn on.

"Hello to the caves. This is Bikini Jones. I heard that some of your children were ill. I'm here to help."

Floating in silence, I watched my holographic display to make sure no Mano were sneaking up on me.

"How did you find this out?" came a deep voice from the cavern.

Time to tread carefully. If I lied to the shark people even once, they'd never believe me again. That's one of the reasons I tried not to lie. Too much of what I do depends on people trusting me.

"I spoke with Matoka. Unfortunately, it was while she was trying to hurt the Mayor of New York City. She is currently incapacitated due to these actions. Her mistake doesn't mean your children shouldn't get help."

"So you've gotten the Voxamatik Corporation to stop dumping their killing chemicals?" The shark man swam out of the cave and I recognized him.

"I'm sorry, Tapedo, but not as yet."

"Then we have nothing to discuss."

"I come in peace. All the Mano can come with me so I can try to help the kids."

"You mean experiment on them. The Mano have had enough of that to last generations. If you're not here to stop the dumping, then we are done talking."

"Tapedo, the shark kids are dying. Are you really going to turn me down?"

"What good is taking the children away to help them if for them to come back and get sick all over again? Unless the threat to our people is ended, it is better for the children to die sooner rather than feebly as false hope is dangled in front of them like a baited hook."

I didn't mean for my throat mike to carry my sigh across the river floor like it did. "You have a point. Show me where they're dumping the material that is hurting your children."

Tapedo swam back and forth for a full minute, his equivalent of pacing.

"Very well. You have helped the Mano before. I hope you will help us now. Follow me," said the shark man as he swam away.

I followed him but could barely keep up and he wasn't straining a bit.

We stopped near pipes that came out of the river floor.

"That is where the toxins are coming from," the shark man said.

"Thanks, Tapedo. Do you want to join me?" I said.

The shark man shook his head. "I would not be able to hide my fury. My attacking and killing these surface scum will only end with them coming in force to kill all the Mano."

"I understand. I'll let you know what happens."

Tapedo nodded and swam out of sight and sensor range.

"Bikini, are you going in there?" came a voice in my ear.

"Yes Aditte, I am."

"Sorry about this Bikini, but you know I have my orders,"

Aditte had outside instructions to protect me from myself, so the mole woman called in the big guns.

Hany had been a slave in the nineteenth century who escaped and spent more than a century on *The Flying Dutchman*. She ran the day-to-day operations of both Bikini Enterprises and The Bikini Foundation charity. She was five shades of amazing and she tried to protect me from the things that came after helping people. "Bikini, you know you can't go around breaking and entering or destroying private property. One, it's against the law. Two, it opens up you and Bikini Enterprises to expensive litigation"

"Hany, it's not that I don't appreciate what you're saying…"

"Bikini, all it takes is one verdict to shut off our cash flow. Then all the good you're doing, all the people you employ, and the major source of cash for your charity goes away."

"Voxamatik winning a lawsuit against me is only a possibility. These shark children dying is a reality. I won't choose money over saving lives."

"What about the lives that will be ruined by becoming unemployed?" she said.

"They'll be alive to get unemployment insurance and find other jobs. I appreciate everything you do to make everything run so I can go out gallivanting, but I won't betray my core values."

I could hear her sigh. "I know, Bikini. Some of us will just have a harder time finding jobs elsewhere." I had aliens, mechanical life forms, and mystical beings on the payroll. But I knew Hany was including herself in her statement. "There aren't a lot of companies looking to hire a woman who is over one hundred and ninety years old."

She had a point. You won't believe how hard it was to get her a social security card. She barely looked twenty-five. Most people would assume she's pulling a fast one with her birthdate.

"Hany, just because they might sue us doesn't mean we can't convince them that it wouldn't be in their best interest," I said. "Aditte, send out one of the probes and have it follow me to measure chemicals, radiation, and anything else that might be coming out of that drain."

A probe about the size and shape of a softball dropped out of the lower bay and headed toward the pipe opening.

"The toxicity in that water is off the charts, especially heavy metals," Hany said, obviously monitoring from the Tower. "The amount of methylmercury is a thousand times the legal limit. That stuff can cause all sorts of central nervous system defects in humans. Since the shark people are humanoid, it's probably doing the same to them, starting with their weakest members first."

"Aditte, send the probe up the pipe."

"Sending probe."

The sphere disappeared through the toxic sludge.

"It leads to a factory and vats," Aditte said. "The probe has left the vats and is in a room."

"There is a Voxamatik logo on the wall and they're stupid enough to label the chemicals with OSHA labels. We have enough evidence to prove it's them," Hany said.

"So any more objections?" I said.

"No. Stop them," Hany said.

I smiled. "Aditte, you know how you always complain I never let you have any fun?"

"I wouldn't say always."

"I want you to fire the plasma cannon on that pipe and fuse it shut so nothing can leak out."

Aditte actually yee-hawed. "Bikini, your wish is my command."

An orange beam shot out from *The Brass Ring* and super-heated the entire opening to molten sludge.

When the river water cooled the plastic and metal, the pipe was sealed.

My holographic display flashed an alert. Something big was approaching me fast from behind.

I spun in the water to see Tapedo approaching. My common sense was screaming to move out of the way of the huge predator but I held my ground.

"Bikini Jones, you have stopped the toxins from entering the river," the shark man said.

"Temporarily. Next, I will work on making it permanent. In the meantime, would you and the rest of the Mano please join me at Bikini Tower as my guests while we arrange for treatment of the children?"

"Will you truly be able to save the children?" Tapedo asked.

"I'm going to do my darndest."

Tapedo looked from me to the slagged pipe, then the shark man bowed. "On behalf of my colony, I accept your offer."

9

Forty-five of the Mano people came with us to Bikini Tower. Nine of them were kids and in horrible shape.

I didn't immediately send Matoka to Rikers Island to be locked up. She did the wrong thing for the right reason so I thought she at least deserved to see that her people would be taken care of.

It was all hands on deck for the Bikini Foundation medical team. In short order we had all the kids hooked up to dialysis and IVs.

Doggy Dr. Dendrite had taken the lead on the treatment front. I was happy he motioned me aside. I was less than thrilled that his tail wasn't wagging.

"Are they going to make it?" I whispered.

"Now even as possibly the world's greatest doctor, I can't promise any results." Since the former super-villain had turned over a new leaf and began working as a consultant for the Bikini Foundation, he'd had lost some of his arrogance. There was still plenty left though.

"But?"

"It looks good. Did you know that the livers of the Mano are very similar to that of sharks? Instead of being the same shape as the human version, they have tubes along the inside of their torsos."

I'd suspected, but I didn't want to get into a long discussion about biological minutia so I just motioned with my hand for him to continue.

"As bad as the damage to their kidneys is, the damage to their livers is even worse. In most typical sharks, the liver makes up around twenty-five percent of the body weight and ninety percent of the space in their body cavity. In an adult Mano, it's maybe eighteen percent, which in this case is a good thing because they were large and strong enough to filter out the methylmercury which stopped the adults from becoming too ill. Unfortunately, the livers of the shark children barely account for eleven percent of their body weight which is why they succumbed to the heavy metal poisoning quicker than their adult counterparts. We got all of them hooked up to IVs for chelation." Dr. Dendrite raised an eyebrow. While he was less arrogant, he never tired of pointing out he was a self-proclaimed mega-genius. While the term was accurate, it didn't mean that Dendrite knew everything.

I had five doctorates, one in exobiology. I knew what chelation was. Basically, we were injecting chemicals into the shark kids' circulatory system that would bond with the methylmercury to prevent any more from getting into their system. With any luck, it might even draw some of the heavy metal out of their organs.

"After we determine when the chelation had reached its maximum efficiency, we will do a blood cleansing." Think of it as a self-transfusion that will take the blood out of a major artery, run it through a filtering machine to clean out the chemicals that are bonded to the methylmercury, and put the clean blood back in. "Gibby—" which is what Dendrite calls Dr. Gibson, an extremely uptight surgeon who, not unlike Dendrite, has an exaggerated sense of self-superiority. The pair had worked together to save a bunch of women whose brains had been stolen by aliens. I'd hoped the experience would give each of them begrudging respect for the other. In fact, it made them friends, something, in my opinion, they both needed. "—and I tried convincing the adult Mano that they should do the same, but they are still struggling to trust surface folk. Not unexpected considering their history. Although I must say these shark people's bodies are works of art. Strong, durable, fast, and able to heal several times faster than humans. The strength is tremendous, and the sense of smell is among the best I've ever measured, although their eyesight is maybe better than a typical human by a factor of three, but I can make improvements on that. They can thrive in fresh and seawater, not to mention air. With a few modifications, it would be the perfect body to place a human brain."

I placed my hands on my hips and glared down at the furry mad scientist who chuckled.

"Not that I'm planning on transplanting *my* brain into a new home anytime soon. After all, my ex-wife isn't likely to let Harper keep a shark man as a pet."

Harper was unaware that her talking dog Mr. Cuddles was, in fact, her father, someone her mother had worked hard to keep her away from. Harper's mother has no idea that Mr. Cuddles can talk.

Harper just thinks she has the coolest dog in the world. The mega-genius is no fool, at least where his daughter was concerned. He knows one day he'll have to tell Harper who he really is.

Dr. Dendrite has done a lot of bad things in his life, the entire litany of which Harper could find with just a single Google search. Showing Harper that he can be a good person even as a dog is pretty much the most important thing in the world to the mad scientist. His daughter looks at me like I'm a hero and even has a poster of me on her wall, which is the main reason why I think Dendrite is helping me and others out.

I'm okay with that. People better themselves for all sorts of reasons. I don't think anyone has the right to judge if those reasons are good or not.

"How's the other project coming?"

Dendrite looked past me. "I think she'd be able to give you a better answer than I can."

I turned my head to see Hany heading my way. "Dr. D, would you do me a favor and give Matoka a medical update on all this? Please offer her the chelation treatment too."

"Is she going to be here that long?"

I shook my head. "I doubt it, but state law mandates prisoners are not to be denied life-saving medical treatment, so we can arrange to do it in the Rikers infirmary if we have to."

Dendrite's canine face grinned. "Excellent. I have some subjective questions on the shark person form I'd love to ask." The mad scientist saw the look on my face. "Purely for research purposes."

Dendrite headed to the containment cube as Hany reached my side. "It should come as no surprise that the CEO of Voxamatik Corp. and his legal team have been calling since the wee hours of the morning."

"Is our little production ready?"

Hany smiled. "I think our PR team has done a brilliant job tying footage from the East River, the factory, and here in the infirmary into a truly heart-wrenching video."

"What about the 47th floor?"

Hany looked at the wooden clipboard that she perpetually carried. Despite being almost two hundred years old, she was good with modern tech but preferred paper to electronics.

"It should be ready before sunset." Hany tended to reference points in time that were more environmentally related than on the clock. "Not that it didn't take a lot of doing. The team should be about done reinforcing the walls and the floor and making them waterproof then backing that up with force fields. Aditte has gone to the upper Hudson River and used *The Brass Ring* to gather up enough clean water to fill the floor you have sectioned off. Although you were right. All of our engineers agreed with your calculations—that much water would put undue strain on the building's structure, so we have several gravity absorbers in place as well."

The gravity absorbers were devices that did just what it sounds like. They absorbed gravity, making the functional weight on the building a fraction of what it should be. It then took the energy from the gravity and converted it into other forms. In our case, it was set for electricity. It was a technology we were gifted with as a thank you the last time I saved Atlantis. They used the things to power the entire city. After all, being that deep in the ocean meant there was an awful lot of water pressure for the devices to convert. "It should be enough to power the entire building as long as we keep it there."

"That's something good at least," I said.

"You've gotten four calls from the police chief, one from a human rights advocate, and two from the Mayor, all of them about you keeping a shark woman prisoner here in the tower. No less than three lawyers left messages that they wanted to talk to Matoka about filing a lawsuit against you for unlawful imprisonment." I looked over to where the shark woman and the dog with a human brain were conversing near nine beds filled with shark children. Matoka was still restrained, but the cube had converted into a chair so she could watch and converse. She wasn't complaining.

"I don't think she's going to sue or press charges against me."

"I know. But if you could, please take care of those issues as soon as possible. It's making Stanley—" my personal assistant. "—a tad stressed."

I had to fight a chuckle. I didn't envy Stanley or Hany having to run interference in order to make what I do possible, but I appreciated it.

"Let me talk to Matoka and I'll have Aditte deliver her to Rikers."

"Do you want Stanley or me to call the mayor and the chief to let them know?"

I shook my head. "I'll take care of it."

"Are we still going ahead with the press conference with the UN?"

"Unless something else major comes up."

Hany smiled and sighed. "I'll put it down as a maybe."

As I got close to the cube chair, doggy Dendrite finished up his conversation and walked away.

I stepped in front of the shark woman but Matoka didn't meet my eyes. "Hi."

Matoka bowed her head to stare at the floor, then up to look at the shark children in their hospital beds before finally turning to me.

"Bikini Jones, I owe you the deepest apologies. You not only stopped the surface people from polluting our water with their poison but you have figured out Mano physiology enough to treat and save our children."

"I like to do the same with the adults. Mr. Cuddles—" Dendrite used his dog name with most people, least Harper overhear someone calling him by his real name accidentally. "—explained everything to you?"

The shark woman nodded. "He did. Are all dogs so smart?"

"No. He's unique as far as I know. Will you take the treatment?"

"I do not know."

"The other Mano look up to you. Perhaps if you talk to them, they might consider it. Hopefully, you will too."

"Bikini Jones, if you tell me it will help us, that is good enough for me. I will forevermore believe you. Thank you for all this. I'm very sorry that I tried to eat you."

"That's in the past. I just ask that the shark people continue to keep their promise to not eat other intelligent beings including humans or pets."

"Is that talking dog the reason why you included pets in our vow?"

"No. I just feel that any animal understanding enough to live with people should be protected as well. It's time for you to go to Rikers Island where you will be arrested and imprisoned awaiting a grand jury. I doubt they will offer you bail."

The shark woman nodded as well as her restraints would allow. "I understand. I must face the consequences of my actions but since my actions saved my people, I will gladly face whatever comes."

"Also, just to let you know I'm in a bit of trouble for keeping you here. The city is claiming false imprisonment and they will probably ask you to press charges against me. You also have no lack of lawyers offering you the chance to sue me for this. What you decide to do with that is up to you."

The shark woman leaned her head back as far as she could and laughed, but this actually sounded like she was amused.

"These foolish humans believe what I would do something against Bikini Jones, the savior of the shark people? Surface folk must be even stupider than I thought."

I smiled. "Thanks for that."

"No, thank you, Bikini Jones. And because of what you've done for my people, I wanted to let you know that there is unrest coming from beneath the ocean floor."

"Seaquakes?" I said.

"Some but there is something dark and powerful struggling to awaken. It is a dark thing that is not only a danger to those of us who live in the water but for those of you above as well."

"Do you know any specifics?"

Matoka shook her head a few inches to either side. "Only what I and others have sensed."

It was cryptic, but that's how these things work. You get some sort of vague warning which later in retrospect makes perfect sense. I'll have Hany contact Atlantis to see if they have any more intelligence on the matter.

I signaled to Aditte that Matoka was ready to go to Rikers.

10

The police chief's face appealed in hologram form above my wrist.

"Hello, Chief. I hear you've been making inquiries about the whereabouts of Matoka. I brought her to Bikini Tower so she could see the treatment is being started on her people."

"I don't care what the reason. I have human and animal rights groups crawling up my butt about falsely imprisoning the shark woman."

"Chief, there was no false imprisonment because, as you so often point out, being a private citizen, I cannot make an official arrest. Matoka has been my guest."

"A bystander uploaded footage of you putting her in that prison pod."

"The shark woman weighs over one thousand pounds. I was hardly going to be able to carry her myself. She was unconscious after our encounter. I wanted to make sure she stayed safe."

"You can't expect me to buy any of that."

"Matoka feels bad about her misunderstanding with the mayor and is on her way to turn herself in at Rikers Island as we speak."

The chief's eyes glinted. "Bikini, you might as well come with the shark woman because I have a warrant for your arrest for unlawful imprisonment."

I smiled. "You've never liked me, have you, Chief?"

"Why would I like a meddlesome self-serving vigilante who routinely makes my department look like a laughingstock?"

"You know I've never heard that from one officer when I arrived on the scene to help them against an acid-spewing experiment that got loose or an invasion by the mole people or alien attack."

"We wouldn't need your help if you'd just hand over your resources like your gadgets and spaceship."

"Sorry Chief, but I don't see you asking other citizens to hand over their property to you. Besides, I've developed, worked for, or negotiated for all of my technology. Your department is welcome to do the legwork to develop the same."

"We don't have the budget for that."

"When I started out, I didn't have any budget. If you want something bad enough and are willing to work for it, then you have a chance of achieving it. Complaining and threatening to steal another person's achievements, especially coming from an officer of the law, is awfully whiny, don't you think?"

"Whiny? You won't think I'm whiny when I come over to Bikini Tower and commandeer that spaceship of yours. As I'm sure you know, police officers can commandeer a vehicle that will help them capture criminals or protect lives."

My smile got even larger. "True enough but the police don't get to keep the car at the end of the chase. And typically when a police officer commandeers a car, they already know how to drive it. Do you know why you don't see police officers commandeering planes and helicopters to chase after criminals? Probably because they don't how to use them and would crash. If I allowed you on the bridge of *The Brass Ring*, you and anyone else you brought would have no idea how to fly it. That means if you tried, you would crash and the resulting property damage and loss of life would be because of your ignorance and arrogance. But if your desire to show me up matters more than a spaceship crashing through a few blocks' worth of skyscrapers and killing tens of thousands of New Yorkers, perhaps you should rethink your career choice. Maybe apply to the supervillain union and see if they'll have you."

I watched as the face of the chief's hologram turned red. He was squeezing his jaw so tight I was amazed he didn't crack a tooth.

When he finally spoke it was in a calm but condescending tone. "The shark woman might press charges if we offer to take some time off her sentence."

I shrugged. "It's up to the DA to make that offer."

"We'll see."

"I don't know how agreeable Matoka will be since she's a trifle furious with the NYPD and the New York State Department of Environmental Conservation for failing to enforce the regulations of the Resource Conservation and Recovery Act. That failure allowed for methylmercury to be dumped in the river, poisoning the shark people. Since there have been multiple cases prior of the NYPD halting dumping in the waters around the city in the past and it has failed to do so this time to protect the Mano that makes it appear that something seems to be causing the inaction. Is there racism against a sister species going on? I wonder what all those inhuman and animal rights activists and advocates will say when they find that out?"

"I'm sure they will be up in arms. Does that mean you will not be turning yourself in?"

"I can if you want. But if you arrest me and Matoka testifies that she wasn't imprisoned, won't that open you up to a false arrest lawsuit?"

The commission sputtered, his spittle turning into holographic fireworks.

"I'll be happy to ask my lawyers for you. They are the best in New York, after all." He just glared. "Tell me now if I should still turn myself in."

After some sexist and unkind curses, the chief's holographic finger slammed down on the button of the holographic phone I gifted to the NYPD and our call ended.

11

"Bikini, I really wish you wouldn't antagonize the police chief," Hany said.

"And I really wish he would get over himself. You know as well as I do it's because I'm a woman. He's said as much to me on more than one occasion. Which isn't very bright as he's got to suspect that I record all conversations."

Stanley knocked on Hany's office door. "Your calls are backing up, Bikini. If you want to have any time to polish your speech before the press conference, you better get them over with."

I stood and looked at Hany. "Duty calls."

A short speed walk by Stanley and a regular one by me later, I was in my office in front of my giant view screen which took up the better part of one of my walls.

"You want the Mayor or the CEO first?"

"Recommendation?"

My assistant raised his eyebrows and smirked. "The Voxamatik CEO is ticked off. The fact that you've made him wait is making him even angrier, so I recommend the mayor first."

I tried to hide a smile. "Just to deliberately annoy him?"

"I saw the list of what they were dumping in the East River and what it did to those kids. That scumbag should be forced to drink that water every day for the rest of his miserable life. Being put on hold is hardly just payback but the only option I have available."

"Works for me. His Honor it is."

Stanley moved to the side out of view and put His Honor's call up on the screen.

"Good morning, Mr. Mayor. I trust you are feeling alright this morning?"

"Only due to your timely intervention. Thank you for saving my bacon yet again."

I smiled. The Mayor was too much of a politician for me to tell if he was being genuine but he was a lot nicer than the police chief.

"I'm always happy to lend a hand."

"You did a heck of a lot more than that. I saw the footage of the fight online. I trust that at the shark woman finally made it to Rikers?"

I nodded. "She turned herself in. I hope you and the DA take into account that while what she did was misguided, dangerous, and wrong, Matoka did it out of concern for the children of the shark people."

The Mayor frowned and nodded. "I'm not going to forgive or forget almost being bitten in half, but your assistant showed me pictures of the condition of the shark children in your infirmary. Terrible business this dumping. And you're backing up the shark woman's claim that it was Voxamatik?"

"It's more than a claim. I have video evidence linking pipes in the East River to vats of toxic chemicals in their factory and samples of the water. I suggest you issue a warning that no one should eat any fish caught in the East River for a long time. Levels are so high it wouldn't have been too long before people on dry land were having problems too. My medical team tells me they are absolutely certain that in a few more days, the shark children would have died."

The Mayor nodded. "As I said, a terrible business but it's going to be awhile before we can even get the company to court to have them cough up enough money to clean up the river."

"Is this further complicated by their rather large donation to your reelection campaign fund during the last election?"

The mayor shrugged. "I won't lie to you. I took their money as well as money from a lot of other companies. I have to have money to get elected. That is how politics work, but I'd also like to point out that they gave an equal amount to my opponent to hedge their bets. That money does nothing to stop my blood from boiling that someone would do this to my city. We both know your hands aren't tied by the same red tape mine are, so if there is anything I can do to help you, just let me know."

I debated about mentioning my issues with the chief but decided not to tattle. "I appreciate that Mr. Mayor, but I think we may already have that covered. Will you still be attending my press conference this afternoon?"

"Of course. The least I can do for the woman who has saved my life eight times."

It was nine, but I stopped one of the attempts before it got anywhere near him so he doesn't know anything about it. "I appreciate it and look forward to seeing you."

The mayor nodded and I heard someone clearing their throat over our connection. The mayor nodded to his side and looked back at me.

"Bikini, would you mind speaking to Officer Carmichael? He was my driver last night."

"Sure."

The Mayor stood and walked off-screen. Officer Carmichael stepped in view, fidgeting so much that he looked like he was wearing sandpaper underwear.

"Hello, Officer Carmichael. Thank you for your help last night, both in getting the mayor out of danger and in loaning me your baton and TASER. Both proved invaluable."

Carmichael looked confused as if he had been expecting me to bark at him like I had last night. I tried not to work like that. Last night was a combat situation with no time for me to be nice. Now I had the time.

"Sure. Anytime."

"I'm afraid your baton is bent and I may have fried parts of the TASER but I'll pay to replace both."

"That was very kind but you won't have to. The department will replace them. I wanted to apologize to you for my actions. I was rude and disrespectful. I also watched the online videos of what happened. I was outclassed from the get-go. That monster…"

"Shark woman," I corrected. "She's a person despite her species and form. Calling her a monster doesn't do anyone any good."

Comical nodded. "Shark woman would have eaten both the Mayor and me. I hope you can forgive me."

"Consider yourself forgiven, Officer Carmichael. You were doing your best to protect someone. I'm sure you would've figured out something. I just have a bit more experience with the weird."

"That's certainly true. I just wanted to let you know that should you ever need one, I owe you a favor."

"I appreciate that."

We exchanged nods and Stanley ended the call

"Ready to deal with the corporate scumbag?"

"Might as well."

12

Kalvin Lackthorne appeared on-screen and greeted me with a rather impressive string of profanity stating in no particular order that I was an excrement-eating, illegitimate lover of dogs, who had intercourse with dead corpses of someone's mother for money.

"I'm rather disappointed by your greeting," I said.

Lackthorne snorted. "Why? Did I offend your sensitive ears?"

"Not in the least but as far as cursing goes it was trite, unoriginal, and quite frankly dull. I suggest you look up Amelia Ehrhardt." The pilot was a big media darling ever since I rescued her from those time-traveling crustaceans. "Now there's someone who can teach you a thing or two about original swearing."

Judging by the ways the muscles in his face fell either he recently had Botox and it just kicked in or my calm demeanor not only disappointed Lackthorne but ruined his plan. You'd be surprised how many CEOs greeted others in attack mode. Typical delusional alpha nonsense. I'd guess he'd planned to make me angry enough to throw me off my game in hopes of making me say something stupid or unkind. I assumed he was recording his end of the conversation as well and had planned to make a creative edit.

"Despite being so predictable and dull, I appreciate that you called as I was going to have to contact you later."

"Why? To beg us not to sue your bikini-covered bottom or to plead with us not to press criminal charges for breaking into our facility and destroying our drainage system?"

"Neither actually. No civil jury would consider what I did criminal. Children were dying because of the toxins you were illegally dumping in the East River so I saw a clear and present danger and stopped your dumping in order to save lives."

"There were no people's lives in danger," Lackthorne yelled.

"Not true. Shark people are people. It's right there in the name. That toxic sludge you were dumping contained over a thousand times the legal limit for methylmercury among other things."

"You can't prove that."

"In fact, I can. While on camera I took samples of the water, sealed them, and sent them to an independent lab to be analyzed. I have video of the entire chain of custody so there is no doubt about when and where the samples came from. My probe also took samples from the vats connected to the pipes in your factory. Again all recorded. The probe did the analysis instantly and which is also included in the footage.

"Your so-called probe broke into and entered my factory."

"In point of fact, it did no breaking although did it enter through an unguarded pipe and unlabeled public danger that was pouring out toxic sludge that was killing people, including children. It was part of my examination as to the clear and present danger. I had to make sure that closing those pipes would not do damage elsewhere."

"Fine, criminal trespass then. You should see the footage we have that thing coming out of our vats inside our factory."

That line was too good to be true. "So you don't mind me having access to and examining your security footage? Thank you."

Lackthorne answered with an even less imaginative string of profanity ending with the word, "No!"

I crafted my question so him saying either yes or no could be loosely interpreted as him not minding. My probe had already connected to his system before it left but I hadn't done anything with the link yet. Too hard to justify any evidence to the authorities.

"Great. I have to put you on hold for a moment." I motioned to Stanley to cut the picture and sound. "Tell our hackers to initiate Operation Toxin." The hackers loved codenames and mission titles. I had given them the link in case we needed something to help the Mano. "I need all security footage immediately, if not sooner."

"On it, Boss," Stanley said.

It took a few minutes, but our white hat hackers managed to copy their entire security footage archive. The connector the drone left there had download speeds designed for the galactic web, the interspatial version of the internet. Ridiculously fast would be slow in comparison.

I suspected we'd have proof shortly.

"Put the evil bozo back on," I said.

"How dare you put me on hold. My time is valuable," Lackthorne said.

"Really? Oh, excuse me, I have something else to take care of. Please hold."

Stanley grinned and did it. "Just doing something to annoy him because you can?"

"Yep." It was petty, but it felt so good. "But it's not all I can do." Hopefully.

"Boss, the hacker squad messaged me," Stanley said.

"What did they say?"

"They are out of energy drinks and snacks but they did a quick analysis of the footage." My hackers are all reformed and skilled. One is even an intelligent computer virus and another is an AI that gained awareness in a machine made by Charles Babbage in 1862, so their skills are on another level entirely. "We have them bringing the chemicals into the factory from a truck labeled as being licensed to legally dispose of hazardous waste. Looks like they were taking money to dump safely and cutting costs by just dumping it in the water and pocketing the difference.

My mental cursing was much worse and more creative than Lackthorne's.

"You want me to add the highlight footage into your special message?"

"Oh yeah. Now put the scumbag back on."

Lackthorne looked ready to spit. "You think that was funny?"

"It amused me."

"Well, see if you're still laughing after this. I expect a check for fifteen million by the end of business today to cover the damage you did."

A second man scooted onto the screen and hovered behind Lackthorne. "What my client means to say, is as his attorney, I'm requesting you pay fifteen million dollars in damages or we will bring you to court and release footage of the damage you did to the public."

"Let me make you a counteroffer, counselor."

The lawyer moved his glasses up on his nose and tilted his head back so he could look down at my picture on his screen. "Ms. Jones, I advise you to have your attorneys make any counteroffers."

"I'll take that under advisement." My attorneys were busy at the moment. "My counteroffer is you shut down the factory, dump the waste you've been paid by others to dispose of like you're supposed to, pay for the cleanup of the neighborhood and the East River, and place twenty-five million in a trust to cover any future medical expenses that the shark people may suffer from the chemicals you exposed them to."

The lawyer laughed. "I'm afraid you're not an attorney, Ms. Jones, and demanding money from my client is considered extortion, which is at a minimum a Class E felony. You could get jail time, starting at four years. Add another five million to the check and we will overlook it."

"So what you're saying is that as far as you are concerned, as a lawyer you can demand money from people with impunity, yet if a regular person does it, you will have them charged with extortion?"

"If it's made in a threatening manner such as you just did, yes. And I did advise you to use an attorney."

"You did, didn't you? Well, then I guess it's a good thing that I am an attorney." I rather enjoyed watching the lawyer's face scrunch up like a human pug.

"It is a crime to misrepresent yourself as an attorney."

"I'm aware. And I'm not misrepresenting," I said.

"That's simply not true. I looked you up, and you Bikini Jones have no law license in New York State."

"You do realize that Bikini is a nickname, not my legal name, right?" By the sudden and slight drop of his jaw, it seemed that the lawyer did not. "You should have checked under Mary Sue Jones where you would have learned that I am licensed to practice law in the states of New York and New Jersey, among other places." (Including a few not even on this planet.)

I don't count my law degree among my doctorates—even though technically it is a Juris Doctor—since it's not commonly referred to as such. I made a deal with a law school to finish the classwork in under a month back before I had much money and needed to defend someone who was framed. The school said it would be impossible, but since I had just stopped a minor Eldritch horror from destroying their campus, they agreed to let me try.

They hadn't taken into account that I have access to a time status chamber that allows me to study within it without aging. I took every test a three-year student would have taken and aced every one of them. Passed the bar on my first try too.

"And since you were so kind as to threaten to charge me with extortion, I want to show you a little something."

I looked at Stanley who nodded that he has finished adding in the security footage, then put a video on the screen that our PR department had been working on all morning. It was great. I'd even done a quick voiceover. Not my best work, but I hadn't had any sleep in over a day.

The video showed the front of the corporate offices. "Voxamatik Corporation took payouts to dispose of toxic waste. Instead of doing what they promised, they ran some pipes into the East River and dumped these toxins into the waters around New York City."

The video pulled back into an aerial view of the factory until the entire city was in the shot. Then it cut to the security footage of the waste coming in and going into the vats and out the pipes, paying the drone's footage in reverse showing the flow to the river.

"The poison they illegally dumped in the New York waterway flowed directly into a small community, sickening their children."

We cut to the ill shark children being taken out of the colony, then them in their hospital beds in Bikini Tower, some of them practically comatose.

"Why did Voxamatik commit such a heinous crime that would have become genocide if not for outside intervention?"

It cut to a picture of Lackthorne at a press conference giving a big thumbs up.

"Only their CEO knows for sure. Hopefully, the authorities will ask him."

The score finished and the screen cut to black, then the CEO and his lawyer reappeared.

"You can't use that. You stole that security footage!" Lackthorne yelled.

"You give me permission just a few moments ago, remember?" I countered.

The lawyer wagged his finger at the camera. "You better not release that or we'll sue you for slander and libel."

"Actually, counselor, as any decent lawyer should know, libel only applies to a defamatory written statement so the video couldn't qualify. Slander refers to the oral variety and that video is neither as I have the evidence to back up everything said."

"I'll have an injunction preventing you from showing that to anyone within the hour."

"We'll have half a million views by then," I said as I smiled and hit a button on my watch. Both men turned toward a rapping at their fifteenth-floor window. They opened the window. Aditte was standing on the hull of *The Brass Ring*, her old school pilot goggles darkened to let her see without pain in the daylight.

Stanley put up footage from her goggles on a split-screen with the webcams. I watched as they foolishly opened the window and she handed each of them the folded paper so that we had video evidence of them being served.

The lawyer stormed back over in front of the webcam. "What is this?"

"I thought it would be obvious to an esteemed member of the bar such as yourself. You've been summoned to court. You have less than an hour to get to the courthouse in Jamaica." The one in Queens, not the Caribbean. "My legal team has petitioned Judge Green for an emergency order freezing all of Voxamatik's assets as well as the CEO's personal ones, to ensure they are available to pay for the cleanup and the damage done to the shark people and their children.

"No judge would do that. There is no precedent."

He was wrong. There was plenty. "You trying to convince me or yourself? Either way, I wouldn't tick off the judge by being late." Which is when an overhead light in the room started blinking. "Bye."

Stanley ended the call. There was only one reason for that light to blink in that pattern.

Someone had broken into Bikini Tower.

13

When I won the tower in a card game from its original owner, it had fifty-eight floors. Currently, Bikini Tower has sixty-two, plus a rather impressive subbasement complex. We have a state-of-the-art security system, but nothing is perfect.

Stanley put schematics of the building on the screen then zoomed in on where the alarm was coming from—a window on the first floor.

"Sherman is already moving to intercept," Stanley said.

Sherman was our octogenarian doorman.

"Let him know him I'm coming down to give him back up. Anything special I should know?" I asked.

"Two life signs. One human, one not."

I nodded and hit a button on my wall. Many corporate heads have private elevators. I had a personal drop shaft which is just what it sounds like. I climbed into a clear crystal canister in a tube big enough to hold a single person and hit a button with the number one. The canister closed and the tube dropped sixty-one floors in eighteen seconds. I palmed the security neural disrupter from the drop pod, making sure it was on its standard failsafe stun setting, and ran towards the side of the building the intruders broke in.

It turns out I could've taken my time. Sherman had a hold of the two intruders by the collars of their jackets and was dangling them about a foot off the ground. Impressive considering each of the intruders was probably taller than him by a good half foot. This was made possible by Sherman's telescoping mechanical arms.

My doorman was a cyborg. He'd been gravely injured defending Bikini Tower from invaders. I called in a few favors. He survived, transformed into an eighty-three-year-old super-strong half-machine/half-doorman. I suggested he retire with a full pension, but he wouldn't have any of it. He still puts in a full week's work.

"Don't worry Ms. Jones, I've got the ruffians well in hand," Sherman said.

"I wasn't worried, just wanted to make sure nothing happened to my favorite doorman."

"No need to worry, Ms. Jones, I can take care of myself."

"I know, Sherman. And how many times do I have to tell you to call me Bikini or Mary Sue instead of Ms. Jones?"

"3342 if we're counting this time. I've offered to call you Dr. Jones, but you said you liked that even less."

"This is great and all but how about putting us down," said a male voice from beneath a familiar hoodie. "I told you old man, I've already met Bikini Jones. I'm sure she was expecting me."

"I'm not sure you sneaking up to the side of a car I was in and whispering through the window at me constitutes an official meeting but I am sure you never made an appointment. I don't appreciate people breaking into Bikini Tower."

"I couldn't exactly come in the front door. We would've been spotted and they would've made us go back," he said.

The girl dangling from Sherman's other wrist spoke up for the first time. "He's telling the truth. We're trying to get away and they'd stop us if they found out."

"You're a couple of teenagers. Who would want to stop you and what are you trying to get away from?"

The young man reached up and pulled down his hoodie, revealing a head covered with gray-green scales and large yellow eyes.

"The Church of the Majestic Deep."

14

I brought them up to my office.

"So the two of you are trying to get away from the Deep Ones' cult?" I said, sitting at my desk facing the two runaways.

"They'd be offended that you called it a cult, but yes," said the girl whose name was Lorraine.

The Church of the Majestic Deep broke away from the Esoteric Order of Dagon a few decades back. Where the Esoteric Order likes to operate on the down low, The Church of the Majestic Deep went in the opposite direction. Taking their cues from some Christian preachers, they went on TV asking for donations and promising salvation. It didn't hurt that they could offer something that most of the other churches couldn't—a chance for cult members' children to live for centuries. They claim immortality, but the oldest Deep One I've ever encountered was barely on the far side of four hundred and fairly decrepit.

Deep Ones are born human. As they hit adulthood, they slowly transform into amphibian humanoids combining the traits of reptiles and fish. Besides being long-lived, they are significantly stronger than a typical human and do as well underwater as they can on dry land.

The Esoteric Order would find married couples and request that one of the Deep One members be allowed to impregnate the wife. The couple would then raise the child as if it was their own and be given special privileges. Back in the old days, that included lots of cash. The Deep Ones had found a sunken ship filled with gold, but that treasure trove ran out back in the sixties. With the loss of that treasure their power lessened and so did the number of men who were willing to allow their wives to get pregnant by someone else.

The Church of the Majestic Deep instead let it be known what the deal was. They encouraged men to join but focused on the women. The ability to mutate into a Deep One is tied directly to the Y chromosome. Female offspring were stillborn. But that also means that in order to continue propagating the race, they had to find women willing to bear their children.

I've dated outside the human species, but Deep Ones have never appealed to me.

Surprisingly, the church took off. Their teachings stressed the fact that the man was the dominant partner in any relationship. I find that a bit abhorrent and ridiculous, but a lot of women were raised that way and buy into that being the way a relationship should be.

The Majestic Deep was successful in recruiting women from other religions with the promise that their children would live forever. Motherly instincts kicked in and many women signed up for the good of their unborn children.

"Let me guess—the two of you found the rules too stifling, especially since you are in love and wanted to run off together."

Judging from the pained expression on Lorraine's face, I'd guessed wrong.

"Ick. Isaac isn't my boyfriend. He's my twin brother."

"I never heard of a female offspring from a Deep One before," I said.

"We're very rare. The doctors think the reason I lived was because Isaac and I shared a uterus and he put out enough hormones or whatever to make sure our mother's body didn't reject me."

"You look about fifteen."

Lorraine shrugged. "Sixteen."

"Which makes Isaac also sixteen. I thought Deep Ones didn't metamorphosize until sometime in their twenties or thirties."

"That's how it used to be, but a lot of us are going through the change as teenagers these days. Our doctors blame it on hormones in the milk and meat which are making us mature faster," Isaac said.

"What made the two of you run off?" I said.

"Our father's a bad man," Lorraine said. "And the bishop of the church."

I raised an eyebrow. "Your father is Braham Leviticus?"

The twins nodded.

"I've heard some rumors, but I have an expert. Would you mind if I gave him a call?" I said.

"Who is your expert?"

"My cousin."

"You said that like we should know who that is," Isaac said, barely hiding that his gaze was locked on my cleavage.

"I just assumed growing up where you did you would have at least heard of Cthulhu Jones," I said.

"Your cousin is *Cthulhu Jones*?" Isaac blurted, his pupils big as dimes.

"Why so shocked? We have the same last name."

"Well, you look nothing alike," Loraine offered meekly.

"You think so?" I teased.

"Well, duh. You look human. Cthulhu Jones doesn't."

"He does favor his dad in looks." My cousin has green skin and tentacles that cover the bottom of his humanoid face.

Loraine covered her mouth with her palm. "That makes Cthulhu—"

I nodded. "My uncle."

"How is that possible?" Isaac said.

"My dad's sister was a little wild." Not to mention dark. "She married Cthulhu." More like became the Bride of Cthulhu. It's a long and twisted story that was rougher on my cousin than on anyone else involved.

"But CJ has moved beyond his past." Mostly.

"Our dad hates him," Loraine said.

"Yeah. He loves telling everyone that the Deep Ones are the sons of Dagon, but that's centuries removed if it's even true. Cthulhu Jones is the son of the most powerful Old One on the planet," Isaac said.

"The Esoteric Order recognizes Cthulhu as a being of worship but our church does not," Loraine said. "For a while, Dad preached that Cthulhu did not exist but your cousin made a liar out of him."

Religious leaders hated that.

"I'm going to get him on the line."

And by I, I meant Stanley.

"Got your cousin. Should I patch him into the hologram projector or the monitor?"

My cousin had a watch similar to mine. "Projector."

An instant later, a larger-than-life hologram flared to life over my desk of a green-skinned man with face tentacles. He was wearing plaid pants and a golf shirt.

"Hey, Bikini."

"Hey, CJ. How are you, cuz?"

"Good, I'm in a golf tournament out here in Arizona."

"I didn't know you played."

"I didn't. Bit of a crash course. Something has been eating the players. The prevailing theory is it's a wendigo. They hired me to stop the murders and figured at the least, my presence might scare it off."

"You need any help?"

"Appreciate it but, nah." His tentacled face turned to look at the Leviticus kids. "I assume you didn't just call to check in. Got problems with my distant cousins?"

"Sort of." I filled him in.

CJ let out a long whistle. "Braham Leviticus is a nasty piece of work. Taskforces have been trying for years to tie him into various fraud schemes and smuggling in everything from ancient artifacts to drugs. There are even whispers of human and inhuman trafficking. The smuggling is easy since his people can all swim deep underwater to avoid the Coast Guard. A single Deep One would show up on sonar as a big fish or shark."

"So the kids' story is legit?" I said.

"Could be. Wouldn't be beyond him to use them as a Trojan Horse if he needed something from you though," CJ said.

"Father's people want to find us and take us home," Isaac said.

"This is our fifth time running away. We were punished severely for the others," Loraine said.

"If they catch us this time, I'm worried they'll do permanent damage. Or worse."

I sighed. "The two of you have put me in quite a dilemma. You're both minors. I can't have you stay here but you can stay at one of the Bikini Foundation's runaway shelters but it would be up to the courts if you have to go back. Do you have any information on any illegal activities your father might be involved in? You could turn that information into the FBI and they could put you into protective custody."

"No. The old fish hasn't trusted either of us since we ran away on our twelfth birthday." Isaac's eyes looked at my bikini top then shot up when he realized I'd caught him.

I fought not to sigh.

"Bikini, my tee time is coming up. Do you need me to head to New York as soon as I'm done here?"

"I think I'm good. Thanks."

Cthulhu Jones waved and ended the hologram call.

"Isn't there any way we could be declared adults and live on our own?" Loraine said.

"I could have you meet with my legal team and see if they can help you build a case to sue for emancipation. And if you don't mind, while you're talking to them, there's a necklace I'd like you to wear." More of an amulet.

"Why do you want us to do that?" Isaac asked.

The amulet was the side effect of a spell someone used a long time ago to make a bunch of people have to lie. They had to take the truth and put it somewhere. That was inside the amulet. It was too late to transfer the truth back, so I use the amulet from time to time. Oddly, it works best on non-humans. A few other issues though. The necklace has to be put on voluntarily or it won't work. It's not admissible in court. And it's only good for three questions.

"Because if you're wearing it, you won't be able to lie."

"I don't like that idea. You could ask me anything I have no choice but to answer." That must have worried the amphibiman teen because he was actually looking at my face.

"It doesn't force you to speak. If you don't want to answer, you just keep your mouth shut and don't say anything. You are asking me to go up against a dangerous religious leader who may be a criminal kingpin and his cult, many members of which have superhuman strength and abilities. If you expect me to go to bat for you, not to mention footing the bill for lawyers and court costs, I need to know that you're on the level. You don't have to wear the necklace. You don't have to answer questions. You can stay in the shelter either way. But I have to decide whether I believe you. Wearing the necklace makes that decision more likely to be the one you want. You can talk it over."

I stepped away to the far side of my office.

The pair seemed to be arguing. Isaac put his arms out to the side to indicate he didn't want to do this. Loraine punched her brother on the arm. He nodded.

Lorraine waved me back over. "We'll do it."

14

The rest of my day flew by until it was time for my press conference. My team set up a podium in the plaza of Bikini Tower.

I had two VIP guests up there with me. The first was the mayor who in the strictest sense didn't need to attend but liked publicity opportunities that put him in a good light. Since it was in my best interest to have a good relationship with New York City—the police Chief withstanding—I tended to include him.

The other VIP was involved with the matter at hand—the Secretary-General of the United Nations.

The Mayor got up and introduced me, then stepped aside from the podium so I could give my speech.

"Ladies and gentlemen let me thank all of you for coming today. The UN and the Bikini Foundation have been working hard to alleviate hunger in some of the poorest parts of the world. What many people don't realize is that these days most farmers in the world buy their seeds from a select few companies. Some of these companies sell patented seeds and demand an agreement that forbids farmers from planting seeds from the new crops so they have to pay them every year for new seeds. Others sell seeds that have been engineered so that the grain, vegetables, and fruit they produce do not even grow seeds. That means there is nothing to grow the next season's crop,

"What this means is, either way, these poor farmers get their first few purchases of seeds at a very cheap rate. Then once they've harvested a few crops, usually enough to make sure they have no other seeds left, the price goes up. They're left with no choice but to buy these new seeds because they have no other way to get any. In my opinion, it is a horrible way to do business with folks who are only trying to feed themselves and their people,

"The Bikini Foundation has been working for years to offer another option. We have developed strains of seeds whose crops will produce patented seeds that we will freely give to allow these farmers to harvest and plant the next year's crops and all the years after that. The first two types of seeds we have ready for mass distribution are rice and wheat,

"Thanks to a grant from the United Nations, we have prepared millions of seeds that we are planning to give to the poor farmers of the world in hopes of giving them the means to build sustainable farming without having to spend all their profits just to have seeds for the next year's crops."

A reporter in the front row's hand shot up. "Bikini, why are these things going only to foreign farmers and not those in the United States?"

"Who says they aren't? The majority will be going to poor nations where hunger and starvation are more of a pressing issue, but many have been earmarked for poor farmers of first world nations including some in the US."

"So why are you anti-business?" asked a blonde woman reporter from a television news channel. "Those seed-producing corporations employ thousands of people. Aren't you taking money from corporations that could cause layoffs for the people who work for them? I mean how are they supposed to compete when you are just giving away something they are trying to sell?"

"These corporations you mentioned have worked for years to develop the dependency of farmers worldwide on them, including those in the United States. They didn't seem to care about all the small and family farms that went under or all those people *they* put out of work, not to mention all the family farms that had to be sold. Was it because it was more important to pay out some bigger bonuses to some executives and a few extra dividends? Where was their concern about the small farmers *they* drove out of business?" The reporter didn't have an answer. "It's been my experience that turnabout can seem very much like justice."

Before I could pick the next question, one was shouted at me by a sadly familiar voice.

"Why are you trying to destroy the moral fabric of America?"

I turned to see the blonde woman who had been protesting outside the Tommy Gunners Bar and Thrill.

I forced myself to smile. "This is a press conference limited to reporters."

The woman smiled at me like she just grabbed the last must-have Christmas toy out of my hands at a Black Friday sale. "I'm not just a reporter. I'm the editor-in-chief of the Deep and Majestic Times."

"So nice that you have a newsletter and think it's the equivalent of the New York Sentinel or ZNN."

The blonde actually had a stenographer's pad and was writing on it with a pencil. "Unlike you and some of my more depravity-leaning colleagues, I believe quality is a far more important attribute than quantity. So, are you going to answer my question about why you are trying to corrupt young, red-blooded American boys, or are you going to continue to hide behind your celebrity status as you attempt to lead this fine nation down the road to becoming the new Sodom and Gomorrah?"

Without losing my smile, I raised an eyebrow, very aware that this would likely be a very big part of the next news cycle. "I didn't hear much of a question there, more of an unfounded accusation, Ms...."

"Not miss, it's Missus. Mrs. Laverne Leviticus."

Great. This kept getting better and better.

"And what you call an accusation, I would say is simply stating the obvious. You parade around immodestly in front of married men and young boys..."

"Let's not forget the women and the unmarried men as well. I go around in front of everyone like this."

That got me a few laughs from the crowd but Lady Leviticus started strutting back and forth like a peacock. "There. You all heard it. She admitted her crimes."

"The way I dress is not a crime. In fact, New York City women, like men, have the right to go topless should they so choose." All thanks to a discrimination lawsuit a while back.

"What else would one expect from such a den of iniquity and sin?"

That got the Mayor's blood boiling and he stood up from his seat on the podium. "Now you just wait a New York minute..."

I lifted my hand so my palm was turned towards the Mayor to indicate that I had the matter under control. At least I thought I did.

"See? She jiggles at the Mayor and he heels like he's her trained dog. No doubt the Secretary-General is similarly entranced. But I'm not and neither are other good, god-fearing women."

"Would that be Jesus or Dagon? Or have you returned to the old ways and upgraded your worship to include Cthulhu as well?" Being venerated as a god amused my uncle by marriage.

"Disparaging my religion! We would expect nothing less from the Harlot of America!"

I've been called a lot of things in my time, but that was a new one.

"We god-fearing people—" I'll admit that worshippers had a lot more to fear from a god-like Dagon than most other divinities. "—see you spitting on the separation of church and state."

"I'm a private citizen, not a government."

"Yet you have representatives of the local government and all the governments of the world here doing your bidding."

"I hardly would call working to eliminate world hunger a bad thing."

"What else would the Secret Queen of the World say?"

I would've liked to have shot back that I wasn't royalty, but in my adventures, I've acquired more than a few roll titles including High Queen of the Lilliputians, Countess of the Parisian Gargoyles, and Princess of Olympus. The last one was an attempt by Zeus to get me to not tell Hera about him making a pass at me while he was in the form of a flamingo. I don't know what the King of Olympus was thinking but I do know that after he didn't take no for an answer, he spent the next few hours curled up in a ball holding his pink feathered groin.

"It's very creative that you make up your own conspiracy theories and have such devotion to trying to convince other people that there's some truth to them. That or you're not quite as in touch with reality as someone living in society should be, so if you're not writing a work of fiction, might I recommend you seek professional psychiatric help?"

"Are you calling me crazy?" she said as spittle flew out her mouth onto the bald head of a reporter in front of her, Poor guy cringed back and pulled a tissue from his pocket to clean off his scalp as he turned and glared at her.

"I'm not comfortable diagnosing you, so I wouldn't say that, but you can feel welcome to. What I'm saying is that what you are babbling on about sounds like the ravings of a delusional individual. And since you haven't even touched on anything related to the topic of this press conference, I'm going to have to move on to other questions."

"You're not fooling anyone, Bikini Jones! We all know that you're trying to seduce men and boys into a life of sin by dressing as you do as well as trying to be a celebrity. You even manipulate the media into helping you distribute images of your harlotry but I'm putting you on notice. The Coalition for the Moral Superiority of America is calling for a boycott of all products and businesses…" She turned to the mayor. "… and places you are associated with. We will be protesting outside Bikini Tower from now until such time as you choose to either admit you're doing wrong or change how you dress."

I shrugged. "As long as you stay on the public areas of the sidewalks and don't harass or block anyone, that's your First Amendment right. I should warn you that this will be taking up a lot of your time because I haven't done anything wrong and I'm unable to change the way I dress."

"Unable or unwilling?"

Ignoring Laverne Leviticus, I pointed to another reporter and took her question instead.

15

"Your press conference is dominating the news cycle but there's not much being mentioned of the free seeds project," Hany said.

"It annoys me that even the news prefers controversy over substance," I said.

"True, but normally your bikini curse works in your favor when you get coverage as the news gets to run stories alongside cheesecake pictures. This time, the bikini is the story. And sadly it seems to be working. We have a sponsor who has broken off their association with you."

"Which one?"

"Zudd Shoes," Hany said.

"After three years of hounding me to have my own line of women's shoes and sneakers? That ticks me off." That deal brought in over twenty million every year, most of which went into the Bikini Foundation. Zudd made out as they could list most of it as a tax deduction because the money was going to a nonprofit. "They want out? Fine. Time for the salted earth clause."

Hany grinned. "I was hoping you'd say that."

I am extremely protective of my image, not just for personal reasons, but because I use my name and celebrity to earn money by endorsing the occasional product. I insist upon a morals clause in every contract. It's so if I find out *they're* doing something unethical, I can invoke it. It's one of the reasons why Zudd no longer uses sweatshops in Asia to produce shoes and instead uses the same people and some machinery that I helped develop and lease to them to pay the workers a decent wage.

I also insist on a dissociation clause. It was not going to be pretty, but I didn't go to them. Zudd Shoes sought me out so they could exploit my name and fame to make money for themselves and their shareholders. During our extensive negotiations, I repeatedly stressed how important loyalty was to me and let them know what I was about and that I expected them to support me. To be fair to them, there was a clause in there to protect their bottom line as well in case another shape-shifting alien doppelgänger impersonated me or I was mystically turned evil again.

The easiest way to handle this would be an apology from their CEO both privately and publicly. We'd consider letting things go back to the way they were. I doubted that would happen.

Stanley stuck his head in the door. "Ladies, I have Mr. Heelth on hold, although he may not realize it yet as I don't think he stopped yelling at me. It seems the Zudd Shoes CEO is a tad upset."

Hany and I looked at each other, lifted our glasses of sparkling water, and clinked them.

"Would either of you like to speak to him?"

"Hany, you start. I want to make a quick call before I get on." I told her what I wanted to do.

I stepped into the hall and called the brownie that'd helped me develop the shoemaking machines which Bikini Enterprises had leased to Zudd Shoes as part of our deal to have them close their sweatshops and pay their workers a decent wage. He was a shoe-making genius and kindly disposed toward me after I'd saved him and his family from an evil cobbler.

When he picked up, my hologram showed me a video screen as he didn't have a holographic projector.

"Hi, Bikini."

"Hi, Aglet. How are your husband and kids?"

"Great. To what do I owe the pleasure?"

"I had a business opportunity I wanted to run by you."

16

When I went back into my office, Heelth was screaming at Hany. "Those fines are extortion. Not only are we not going to pay you anything but we're going to sue you for breach of contract."

Hany grinned. "You're welcome to try but we have video of the contract signing where not only did you have the separation clause explained to you but agreed to it before signing on the dotted line."

"You think there is a contract I ever signed that can't be broken? Zudd Shoes is going to crush you so badly that six months from now, no one will even remember the name Bikini Jones."

I stepped into view. "Now, now, Heelth. That sounded very much like a threat."

"Good, then I made myself perfectly clear."

"So I take it that you have no interest in apologizing and telling the public that dropping me from your sponsorship was a mistake on your part?"

"Hell no. If anything, our PR department will devote itself to smearing your good name."

My shoulders move towards my ears. "Do what you want, but I have one of the best legal teams on the planet. The same planet that I have saved multiple times. Look forward to libel and slander lawsuits against you and Zudd Shoes."

"Maybe you stopped some aliens once upon a time, but we're the fifth biggest sneaker company in the world with revenues expected to reach five billion this year. You don't stand a chance against us so just drop your demands that we pay any fines and maybe we'll just be kind enough to pretend that you don't even exist."

I put my hand on my chest and opened my mouth. "How gracious of you. Let me think about that." I crossed my arms over my chest and stroked my chin with my right hand. "Nope. We are within our legal rights to remove the equipment since you refused to pay the daily rent."

"All this because we canceled our endorsement deal? We wanted you because of your wholesome family image which is something you no longer possess. You are the one in violation of the contract."

"Nothing about who I am or what I do remains has changed. You just chose to listen to someone screaming and complaining rather than looking at the facts and used that noise as a reason to cancel our contract. And the previously quoted fee for our shoemaking machines is no longer in effect. Effective now you will be paying the full rental price for each machine." I quoted him the amount.

"That's a ridiculous price. We will go back to using workers like we used to."

"That is of course your option, but we both know these machines allowed you to keep the same amount of people you are employing and produce three times the number of shoes in the same timeframe. And the shoes are of a much higher quality. If you refuse to pay the rent, as per our leasing agreement, I will have no choice but to immediately pull the machines from your production line."

Heelth, probably trying to be intimidating went with a maniacal laugh but it was just sad. "Fine. We just won't pay and we'll *keep* the machines. Good luck getting them back. As of right now, you are persona non grata on any property that Zudd Shoes owns. Should you or anyone under your employ try to come in to take the machines, they'll be arrested for trespassing. You want them back, sue me. It will be years before you see even one. And since we no longer have to follow the dictates of your stupid contract, we are going to lower the Vietnamese workers' pay down to where it was before our association with you, which means we'll be making three times the shoes for a third of the price. As we no longer have to pay our endorsements to you, adding all these savings together is going to thrill my stockholders."

I motioned to Stanley who came over so I could whisper in his ear. "Initiate Trojan Shoe Protocol."

Stanley gave a little jump and a clap and almost skipped out of the room.

"We expect you to follow the separation clause in the contract as well," Hany said.

"Of course, we'll stop making the product. Interestingly enough, we just produced the entire line for next year."

Heelth was lying. He knew it and I knew it. I also knew he

hadn't talked to his legal team about our contract.

"A pity you'll have to destroy all those shoes then," Hany said.

"Nonsense. We have the right to sell out all of our existing stock. It's in our standard contract."

"We didn't sign your standard contract. You signed ours," Hany said. "If you will review our separation clause, it states specifically that you have seventy-two hours to pull all merchandise off of every store shelf in the world. In hour seventy-three, daily fines for each product in each store begin accumulating. You will have to pay the fines weekly. Failure to do so will invoke the penalty payment section of the clause. This will effectively double the amount owed each week."

"That's not enforceable."

"I believe you'll find it is," I said. "It also states that you will have to pay any and all expenses in my enforcement of the clause including but not limited to legal fees. It also states you have to destroy any unsold product rather than remaindering or giving them away."

"That's ridiculous. It would take us weeks to remove those products, let alone get them shipped back to us. The expense involved would be prohibitive."

"Not my problem. I'm surprised you didn't have your lawyers review the contract with you prior to severing our agreement. At the start of our agreement, I made arrangements with the chains and independent stores that sold the shoes bearing my name and they will be sending me reports about how long these products remain with them before being shipped back so we have an accurate number for the penalty price.

"Fine, we'll make up the difference by lower wages even further and making our Vietnamese factory employees work around the clock to make up the differences in their salaries."

"With what machines?" I asked.

Heelth shook his head. "I never took you for a dumb blonde, Jones. Weren't you listening? You're banned from our factories so you can't get your machines back without being arrested."

Stanley leaned in my office, smiled, and gave me a wink.

"I think you'll probably be getting a call from your Vietnamese factory any moment now." As if on cue, a corporate toady ran behind the desk and whispered to Heelth.

"The machines did what?!"

I smiled. I have access to much more interesting and exoteric technology than most of my competitors. I made assurances that no one is going to keep something I developed if they broke their deal with me. The shoe-making machines flashed and announced in Vietnamese and English for the surrounding workers to back up. Once their sensors showed that was no one nearby, armor plating, strong enough to withstand a rocket launcher, snapped into place around them. This was followed by telescopic robot legs lifting the machines off the floor and marching out of the building.

Hany turned her screen towards me which showed the shoemaking bots' cameras recording security guards trying to stop them to the point where some of them hopped on top and they were all simply carried out of the building. As they marched out, they announced to the workers that the machines would no longer be able to be used at that factory but that Bikini Enterprises would continue to pay their salaries until a new solution had been found.

"You stole those machines from us!"

I shook my head. "I can't steal something I own. As I stated when we first began doing business, I record all interactions. I issued proper notice to you as per the conditions in our contract after which you threatened to keep my property. In order to protect myself, I had my machines remove themselves from your premises to a public thoroughfare."

"I will destroy them before you can get them."

I snorted. "You're adorable. Do you think you actually have something that can break through that armor plating? It's based on the armor used by the Technolot Knights. Clubs, axes, and explosives aren't going to even scratch them."

Stanley ran into my office holding a tablet. "I narrowed down the potential properties to two." My assistant swiped through pictures of the pair of choices before me.

"The first one."

Stanley smiled. "I figured that'd be your pick." He took the tablet from me and switched to a different window and the signature end of the contract. "Legal's been through it. It's a six-month lease with an option to renew or buy and a cancelation clause invalidating it for misrepresentation in case the physical plant is not consistent with the photos. It's all yours if you sign on the dotted line."

"You don't even have the courtesy to wait to conduct your real estate deals until we're done?"

I held an index finger up to the screen, then used it to sign the contract. "This ties in with our conversation. I just leased a factory across town from yours and my machines are going to march their way over there. Before they do, they will make offers to all of your employees to work at the new factory for the new holder of the rights to make Bikini Jones shoes, sneakers, and socks. I expect in the next few days I'll be getting some more endorsement deals from some well-known people. Your company had been poised to make five billion, but I am now part owner of something that is going to make the finest mass-produced footwear in human history. I suspect we're going to take more than a bit of your market share, all because you listened to some screaming woman who was upset over what another woman was wearing. Good luck explaining this situation to your shareholders as our press release should go out within the hour, detailing how your actions led to this development."

Heelth froze like a harpy watching music videos. "Let's not be so hasty about this, Bikini. That one factory accounts for sixty-four percent of our entire production. Without it, we won't be able to fill all the orders we have."

"And you won't be able to fill any of them for any of my products."

The shoe CEO waved a dismissive hand at the screen. "That's maybe seven percent of our total business."

"Seven percent that you have to recall and refund the money for. I think I've shown that I don't bluff so rest assured I will enforce the separation clause until the fines are paid."

"Bikini, perhaps I acted hastily. Maybe we could take a few steps back and revisit everything."

"I don't think so."

"Look, Bikini, I'm sorry. Maybe I reacted poorly to the threatened boycott, especially since Reverend Braham Leviticus made a personal appeal advising me that it would be in my company's best interest to go along with the boycott."

"When did this happen?"

"Over a round of golf."

"The next time you shoot eighteen holes with him, see if he'll loan you the money to make up for your losses."

"Okay, I deserved that. Just because our old deal's gone doesn't mean we can't make a new one. We've got distribution channels set up all over the world. We'd be happy to act as distributor for your new shoe lines. Maybe even hire your factory to manufacture some of ours."

"Nope. When people see the quality of our shoes combined with the media blitz we're going to do, distribution won't be a problem. I just don't see the point of letting you take any share of that, especially after your personal betrayal of me. I wish you well in your future endeavors. I advise you not to be late with any penalty checks. Have a wonderful day."

Heelth's smile went into overdrive as if he was trying to charm a Cobra Naga into not swallowing him for dinner. "Bikini, I think we can chalk this up to a horrible misunderstanding…"

I nodded to Hany who ended the video call

"I guess your brownie friend agreed to go into business with you?" Hany said.

"More like allowed me to go into business with him. It'll take a little creative bookkeeping and money shifting, but I should have enough funds to put up operating expenses for the next nine months by which time money should be pouring in." Hopefully. "Hany, Stanley, I want you both to get to work with PR to spin this and make Zudd look bad and us look good. Make sure it sends a message to anybody else who is thinking of joining this bikini boycott," I said. "I need you to send our business development team to Vietnam immediately to get this factory up and running as quickly as possible. Have Aditte take them over on *The Brass Ring*."

Stanley went out to make the arrangements.

"Now with that crisis averted, did you have a chance to talk about the runaway situation?" I asked.

Hany nodded. "I did. It's just as you suspected. Not only is Laverne Leviticus the prime wife of Braham Leviticus…"

"Prime wife?"

"Their religion allows for polygamy. Prime wife simply means that she is first among all his wives."

"How many does he have?"

"Eighteen, although it's more of the title than a legal ceremony. By not legally marrying any of them, he's not breaking any marriage laws but by making it a religious title, he's able to get all the benefits of multiple wives with none of the drawbacks like divorce or need for prenups."

"Sounds like a lovely gentleman."

"Not. And Laverne is the mother of our two runaways. According to the twins, her amphibiman husband is rather enamored of you. She walked in on him doing some intimate self-activities while watching one of your movies on his computer."

"Ick." I didn't even want to know which one. They are all PG-13.

"And her son has your latest calendar up on his wall which she had issues with before catching her husband."

"So that's why she's waging this boycott?"

Hany nodded. "It appears to have triggered her. Quite successfully if this conference call was any indication. Protestors have taken up spots in front of Bikini Tower and are harassing anyone going in or out. When they have nobody to harass, they're calling you the harlot of America and chanting 'Ban Bikini Jones.'"

Wonderful. This was giving me a headache. I rubbed my temples and thought about the situation.

I didn't win against superior foes because I was stronger. I did it by thinking outside of the box and I would have to do that here. "I think I'm going to go pay the protesters a visit."

"Is that even safe?" Hany said.

I spoke with a confidence I didn't really have. "What could go wrong?"

17

"How's everybody doing today?"

The crowd of protesters all stopped in their tracks. They hadn't been expecting me to come out a side door and suddenly pop up in the middle of the group. It didn't hurt that I was trained in the hilarity of unseen sneakiness by the Clown Ninja Monks of Newark. They should all consider themselves lucky to have avoided a pie to the face, a squirt with a seltzer bottle, or a hot foot.

Most of the protesters were stunned into silence except one. She screamed from being startled by my sudden appearance.

I smiled. "Thanks. It's nice that you are so excited to see me."

The woman actually smiled back.

Luckily the first Mrs. Leviticus was nowhere to be seen. Maybe these protesters would be more reasonable to talk to.

"So the Harlot of America dares to show her face," said a woman with brown hair. From my observations through the security cameras, she was the one leading the chanting.

"Whether I am celibate or enjoy my love life to excess, it's frankly none of your concern. And I dare to show a lot more than just my face." I motioned my hands towards my body and even did a little spin which is when I noticed the reporters covering the protest had stopped acting bored.

"How dare you parade around in front of us dressed like that," said the brunette.

"A witch cursed me to always wear a bikini. If I put anything on over it, it vanishes."

"Fake news propaganda made to excuse your slutty behavior to the masses."

"Nope. Would you like me to prove it?"

The protesting women exchanged glances with each other as I wasn't shaping up to be the monster they were told I was.

The brunette grinned. "Sure, but you can't prove the impossible."

"You'd be surprised. Does anyone have an item of clothing that they would be willing to part with so I can buy it off them?"

A short woman pointed to her chest where she wore a white T-shirt with black letters that spelled *Boycott Bikini*. "I'll give you this T-shirt for twenty bucks, an autograph, and a selfie."

The brunette's face scowled and she wagged her finger as if she were scolding a child. "How dare you betray the cause and fraternize with the whoring enemy!"

"I think what you told us in our church group is wrong. She seems very nice and it's not like she's wearing a string bikini and a thong."

Not a week goes by that I thank my lucky stars that I wasn't sunbathing topless in my parents' backyard when Mrs. Doomhilda's pervy husband pulled his Peeping Tom act on me. The witch didn't do anything to him, but me she curses to wear only a bikini for all eternity and until she started screaming at me, I hadn't even known he was there.

Hardly fair but it has helped me to have an interesting life.

I wore a gauntlet on my right wrist with a pouch that served as a wallet. I pulled out a twenty and the woman shimmied out of the shirt—she had another underneath it—and we made the exchange. Then I signed and personalized an envelope in her purse—her name was Debbie—and then we took a couple of selfies, one on her phone and one on my watch.

"You mind if I tweet the photo?" I asked.

Debbie's grin grew even larger. "You'd do that? Wait until I tell everybody in my carpool!"

Sherman came out the front door rolling a cart over to the crowd.

"Before I do my demonstration, I imagine being out here standing on your feet and holding up signs must be tiring work." Especially since most of them were in not so sensible heels. "On behalf of Bikini Enterprises, my friend Sherman here and I would like to offer you snacks and beverages if you'd like some. We've got soda, water, sandwiches, and chips, including vegan options. And since it is a little chilly out here—" Trust me, I notice these things for obvious reasons which is why my watch sported an area heating unit. "—we have coffee, tea, hot chocolate, and espresso. Please help yourselves."

I guess none of the organizers of the protest had given much thought to their demonstrators because the ladies all put down their signs on the sidewalk and approached the snack cart like a swarm of locusts. All except the brunette.

"Don't think you can buy our morality by bribing us with a few morsels of food."

Debbie gave a little squeal. "They have crab cake sandwiches. I love these."

Sherman walked over to the head protester, all five foot three of him looked up at all five foot nine of her.

"I don't understand what you have against Dr. Bikini Jones." I had to smile. He finally used my first name, even if it wasn't to address me. It didn't slip by that he also used Dr. instead of Miss, trying to build up my importance. It's not that I think getting a doctorate makes someone better or worse than someone else, it just means that person was willing to put a lot of work into getting that degree. Which was why some people place a lot of weight on someone being called doctor.

"Isn't it obvious?" she said.

Sherman shook his head. "Not at all. She's a brilliant woman, the best boss I've ever had, she keeps people safe, and runs a charity that does nothing but help people who need it. There are no problems from what I can see."

The brunette tilted her head and gave Sherman the stink eye. "Exactly. You judge her by what you can see, which is pretty much everything because you're a dirty old man who enjoys looking at a mostly naked older woman." Ouch. I was only 29. "And that's the core of the problem. She prances around…"

"Oh come on now. When has anyone ever seen me prance? Sure, maybe there was that one time in the second grade Christmas play, but what was I supposed to do? I was actually playing the part of the reindeer Prancer." (Who's a magically intelligent flying deer and a very nice guy.)

The brunette took a deep breath and plunged forward, ignoring what I said. "She distracts men and gives them lascivious thoughts, tempting them to engage in premarital sex, adultery, and self-gratification."

"Dr. Jones does not create those thoughts or urges. If seeing her in a bathing suit brings thoughts like that to the surface of someone's mind, that person has poor moral character and even worse self-control. Not to mention a lack of respect for women," Sherman said.

I couldn't stop from grinning. Sherman was demonstrating

one of the many reasons the cyborg octogenarian was one of my favorite people in the world. Several worlds in fact.

"Nonsense," the brunette said. "A man is not to blame for his reactions to her nearly naked body. The fault lies solely with her. I would go so far as to say that anyone who dresses so provocatively, even at the beach or pool, is a degenerate slut."

I was about to say something about slut shaming when Sherman not only beat me to it but made all conversation stop and jaws drop as he slipped off his full-length red doorman uniform by undoing one gold button at a time before finally sliding it off and folding over his arm like a maître d' carrying a towel.

To say Sherman was out of uniform was an understatement. He was dressed in what looked like a red castoff of one of my bikinis. Since I couldn't re-wear them, I put my castoff tops and bottoms in a box in the office closet and made it clear that any staff member who would like one of their own was welcome to it provided they weren't doing something creepy with them or selling them online.

Sherman is shaped a bit like a baked potato. And like a baked potato, parts of him were covered—not in aluminum foil but by shiny metal components over much of his arms, legs, and parts of his torso. He had augmentation in his head but that the techno-surgeons were able to cover with his own cloned skin cells. Body parts like livers and skin are cloneable, but it's rare to successfully clone a stable human body that develops any faster than a normal human. It's one of the reasons Jenny has an alien body instead of a cloned one.

Sherman was offered the opportunity to have the rest of him covered in skin but turned it down. He liked the way he looked and I must admit he cut quite an intimidating figure considering his body shape, the fact that he was only wearing a red bikini, the black boots from his uniform, and his doorman hat.

"Well if Dr. Bikini Jones is a degenerate slut, then I'm quite proud to say so am I."

Sherman leaned toward me, gave me a wink, then whispered, "I got the inspiration from your large gangster friend. I hope you don't mind me taking this out of the giveaway box. I did take it home to have the missus let it out in a few places so it fit me. "

"You're perfectly fine. Thank you." I leaned in and kissed him on the cheek and even the cybernetics couldn't hide his blush.

"How you dress is a choice that you made and that she makes every day," scolded the brunette, again wagging her finger, first at the doorman and then at me.

It was the perfect time to get back to what I was originally going to do.

"And here's where I prove to you that I have no control about wearing anything other than a bikini. If I could interrupt everyone's snack for a moment and have your attention."

The protesters' pupils all went wide when Sherman took off his coat so I knew they'd been paying attention even if they were pretending not to. The camera people weren't even trying to pretend.

Positioning myself so the camera people (not to mention our security cameras) could get a good shot, I held the shirt between my hands so it covered the front of me. "This is what I have to say to the Boycott Bikini protest."

I pulled the T-shirt over my head, put my arms through the sleeves, then pulled it down past my waist.

"It's about time you covered up, you sick and shameless hussy! You've only proved that you could have done this at any time instead of trying to seduce all the menfolk—" Yep, she said menfolk. "—in this country, and in fact the entire world."

I shot her a look. "Wait for it."

The amount of time it takes for clothing to disappear off my body varied from a few seconds to almost two minutes. I have a bit of control over slowing the process and my record is two hundred and seventeen seconds. This time I didn't try to slow the disappearing and instead used the opportunity to change my bikini. As I've said, if I focus hard enough, I can control what kind of bikini reappears on me, and this time I made it a red one to match Sherman's.

I felt the tingle of the magic and the shirt disappeared entirely.

I turned to face the brunette. "And that's why I can't wear nice, normal clothes."

"It's a magical disability that Dr. Jones has," Sherman said, wagging his own finger at the brunette. "So I guess that makes you a bully who liked to pick on people with disabilities, doesn't it, young missy? Shame on you." His finger swept over all the protestors. "Shame on all of you bullies."

The brunette stammered. "I have nothing against the disabled.

I have friends who are disabled. This is a moral issue."

"So it's morally just to pick on somebody with a disability?" Sherman said. "Who's next? Kids in wheelchairs? The blind? Me because I'm an old man with most of his body made out of metal? Are you going to make fun of my disabilities next? What a horrible nasty person you are! Why anyone would take you seriously is beyond me. Bullies like you disgust me." Sherman looked at his watch. "I need to get back to my post." The bikini-wearing senior walked over to the food cart. "Grab any last-minute snacks, ladies, as I have to take this back in."

More than half the protesters grabbed something else to eat or drink.

"I've hoped you've all learned your lesson and are not going to behave poorly like that nasty bully over there."

The protestors saw the cameras turn towards them and again exchanged glances with each other.

Debbie became the new spokesperson for the spinoff group. "No, of course not. We thought Bikini was doing it on purpose. We had no idea she was cursed or anything. We're going to leave right now."

"Right after we finish this food," said another woman who had a cupcake in each hand.

Sherman left with the cart and I followed.

"I have to be getting back to work myself. It was nice meeting you ladies," I said facing the group who was still noshing. Then looked back over my shoulder at the brunette. "Most of you at least."

"It was great meeting you, Bikini. Thank you so much for the selfie and the autograph," Debbie said.

"Thank you so much for having an open mind and a frank discussion with me."

I turned and walked away, fighting the urge to prance into the building just to spite the brunette.

18

When I came in to work the next day, Sherman was standing at his post wearing a bikini, although he wore his red doorman long coat open in front.

It looks like the first wife had suckered in a new batch of protesters that was triple the number of the last. The brunette was the only one who had returned from yesterday.

I didn't have the time or the inclination to do a repeat performance so I tried to simply walk through the crowd but they weren't having it. The group phalanxed up, blocking me from Bikini Tower, screaming out their chants. Honestly, I think I'd be dating a lot more if I really was the Harlot of America.

"Good morning, ladies," I said, trying to be nice, but these women were hardcore and weren't having any of it. They just chanted louder. Or maybe it seemed that way because the brunette and a few others pulled out bullhorns.

Yesterday's mediation had been a good part of the news cycle so today there were more reporters and more camera people so it would be a really bad idea to try any threats.

I weaved left, then right, but they blocked my path. This was stupid. Time to go around the corner and call Aditte to pick me up.

That's when Sherman blew on the whistle he used to call cabs for people. Instead of the usual double whistle, this one had five short screeches which was followed by him opening the lobby door.

Considering all the wild things I've seen and done over the years, it's hard to surprise me. Not only was I surprised, I was confused, at least for the first second. I watched as Hany and Stanley marched out of the building. Instead of Stanley's business casual and Hany's CEO chic, they each wore bikinis. Dozens of my employees, including Aditte and Dr. Gibson, followed them. However, one employee truly stood out from the rest—Jenny.

Her unusual appearance made the phalanx of protestors scatter as she floated through the air, her tentacles lazily skittering along the ground. Jenny had been a victim of aliens who just about conquered the Earth when the ancient Egyptian Empire was the major power on the planet.

They were defeated by removing part of their brains and locking them in a pyramid outside of Philadelphia, PA. An evil sheriff freed them and set up women to have their brains taken by the aliens. The SOB shot Jenny's brainless, but still living, body, killing it.

Dr. Dendrite had managed to return the other victim's brains to their bodies, but the bullet had destroyed Jenny's brainstem—the only part of the brain the aliens left behind. To make the long story about the brainnappers from outer space short, she ended up getting control of the alien body, complete with one huge cyclopean eye, green skin, and plenty of tentacles.

And yes, she too was in a bikini which was rather impressive considering she had none of the body parts a bikini was designed for.

Now that the herd of woman protesters had made like the Red Sea when Moses showed up, my phalanx of bikini-clad employees split into two row and surrounded me. Just by pointing her finger, Hany got the group to do an about-face and we marched to the front doors as cameras flashed, taking pictures of nearly fifty of my employees of every gender and many species escorting me into the building.

I found myself smiling. It was going to be a great day.

19

My first clue that I was wrong about the great day thing was the police chief and two officers storming Bikini Tower demanding I present myself to be arrested.

Sherman refused to step aside and none of the officers wanted to be caught by the surrounding news cameras roughing up an eighty-plus-year-old man, which left the police chief with few options. He chose to just keep yelling louder.

It prompted two very different reactions from my two closest coworkers.

"Bikini, run. I'll cover for you," Stanley said.

Hany crossed her arms over her chest and started tapping one of her feet. "What did you do now?"

"Nothing arrestable unless Matoka changed her story." Which I didn't think was very likely. "I guess we'll just have to wait and see. Tell Sherman to let them in."

Even though the doors to my office were in the half-open position, the Chief rushed through them, slamming one against the wall.

"Good morning, Chief Flag."

"What is wrong with everybody here? What in blazes are all of you wearing?"

None of my staff had taken off their bikinis after escorting me in. Stanley suggested we do it regularly and call it Bikini Tuesday. I was honored and touched. Not coincidently, my giveaway box of old bikinis was just about empty.

"What do you mean?" I said with feigned obviousness.

"What you and your band of freaks are wearing doesn't matter." The chief had the most self-satisfied smirk I'd seen on a human face in quite some time. "Bikini Jones, you are under arrest."

"On what to charge?"

"Two charges of kidnapping a minor. You have the right to remain silent..." I was a good enough lawyer to know that was excellent advice. Despite what you see on TV shows and movies, if you are ever arrested by the police keep your mouth shut and don't say anything except you want an attorney.

After he finished Mirandizing me, Flag grabbed my shoulder, spun me around, then slammed me face-first on my desk. This was followed by handcuffing me.

"Take your hands off her," Stanley yelped. "That's police brutality!"

"Shove it up your girly…" The Chief stopped speaking when he realized that Stanley had his phone out and was recording.

The Chief held out his hand. "It's illegal to record the police chief performing his duties. Give me the phone."

"So you can delete the recording?" Stanley laughed. "You're old and slow, Officer Fossil. We're live streaming."

"And your line about recording is not true, Chief. And it wouldn't matter because you're being filmed by our security cameras as well," Hany said.

Stanley gave me a look, then pointed with his eyes to my drop tube. I shook my head. I had a pretty good idea where this was headed and I tried not to fight officers of the law who were just doing their duty. It's the other kind I caused trouble for.

We went down the main elevator past Sherman who had such a dejected and helpless look on his face that it made me want to cry. The chief strutted, holding my elbow as he perp-walked me out of Bikini Tower to a waiting squad car in front of all the reporters to the cheers of the protesters.

As I was perp-walked into One Police Plaza, there was a mixture of looks on the police officers' faces. Most were confused, while a few had smirks on their faces.

Fingerprinting was easy—they just scanned my fingertips.

It'd been a while since I'd been arrested so I debated about how I should pose for the mugshots because I knew within an hour they'd be leaked to all the tabloid news sites and the Internet.

I went with a slight smile. Too big and I wouldn't look as if I was taking things seriously. If I looked scared or sad, people might think the charges had some validity. I held the number plate in front of my chest after deactivating my photo obscuring earrings.

The Chief was no dummy so he then confiscated my watch and my earrings.

Then the Chief had a couple of officers take me into an interview room and handcuffed me to the table. They left me to cool my heels.

I had other ideas. It took me maybe fifteen seconds to get the handcuffs open, after which I ran my fingers through my hair. I leaned back in the chair, put my feet on the interview table, and my hands behind my head. I knew the Chief and probably some others were watching me through the two-way glass and knew my lack of worry and defiance of how prisoners should act would only serve to tick the Chief off.

I was impressed because the Chief didn't storm in and start yelling at me but instead let me stew for twenty minutes. As he opened the door I smiled, sat up, and put my hands back in the cuffs. If I didn't do it as if I was someone guilty who had gotten caught but as if I was humoring someone who was as petty as a spoiled child.

"You really stepped in it now, Jones. I knew you were no good and if I waited long enough, I'd nail you."

"You're not my type, Chief, and that type of talk is derogatory to women."

"Dammit, you know I didn't mean it like that. So do you want to do this easy way and confess to the kidnapping of the Leviticus twins? Or do we go through this the hard way? It doesn't matter to me because they both end with you going away for a long time. So what'll it be?"

"I am invoking my Fifth Amendment rights and requesting an attorney before answering any questions."

"So you're going that route, ha? The way of the guilty. We both know we don't have to wait. You're an attorney and since you're here, why not represent yourself and get this over with?"

Although I have been forced to represent myself several times in courts in many jurisdictions and a few worlds, I still believed in the adage that only a fool has herself for an attorney. "I would like my attorneys," I reiterated.

"We can do this all day," Chief Flag said. Which from a legal point of view was incorrect. Once I'd requested an attorney, all questioning should have stopped until I got one. In case my first statement was unclear, I repeated myself and added that he was now violating my civil rights.

Flag ignored my request and my civil rights for several more minutes until I heard a commotion outside the interrogation room.

I heard several voices saying "You can't go in there!"

A deep booming voice in what approximated a British accent respond, "My client is in there being illegally questioned so I can assure you, I have every legal right to enter the room along with my partner who is recording this interaction. We already have enough for an impressive lawsuit against the NYPD. If you would like to continue to hinder my entrance, I would be happy to add another zero to the lawsuit as well as all of your names. If not, then kindly step aside so I can do my duty as an officer of the court."

I recognized the voice and knew he could be quite intimidating without any legalese. That someone who looked like him spoke it fluently probably confused the officers outside.

When in doubt, kick it up the chain of command. An officer cracked open the interrogation room door and said, "Chief, there are…"

Which is when an arm the size of a small tree trunk reached over the officer's head and pushed the door open all the way. The arm's owner walked past the cop as if he were nothing more than a plastic bag floating in the wind. The ogre had to duck in order to fit through the door.

"Shrill and Crunch, attorneys for Dr. Mary Sue Jones," Crunch said in an extremely deep and well-cultured British accent. "You will cease all questioning immediately."

A rather curvaceous, obviously mechanical woman in a black business suit with a white blouse which was every bit as nice as the gray suit, white shirt, and red tie that Crunch wore, followed him in.

The Chief looked up and glared at the huge ogre who just entered the interrogation room.

"Who the blazes is Mary Sue Jones?"

"That is the proper and legal name for the woman you have arrested," purred Shrill in a melodious voice too perfect to be organic. "Are you even sure you have arrested the correct woman as you don't even know the name of who you are detaining? A warrant made out for the arrest of Bikini Jones would not be valid."

"I'm doing more than detaining. She's under arrest."

"So I've heard, on a fabricated charge of kidnapping," Crunch said, seating himself beside me. Not in a chair but on the floor. His head was still higher than mine. Shrill took up the chair to my other side.

"I assure you there is nothing fabricated or trumped-up regarding this most heinous crime," Chief Flag said.

"Why don't you give us the details that you're charging our client with, Officer," Shrill said.

The Chief took the bait. "My rank is not officer."

"My apologies for the mix-up, Sergeant."

"I am the police chief of New York City."

The android and the ogre leaned forward and looked at each other and then back at the law officer.

"I'm afraid that seems highly unlikely given the nature of these charges, I'm afraid." Shrill said.

"I'm forced to agree. The person who holds such a critical office in the greatest city in the world would have to be far more knowledgeable in the workings of the law than you've shown thus far," Crunch said.

"Exactly. I'm afraid we need to see some sort of identification to verify your claim," Shrill said, the glowing orbs on her faceplate that passed for eyes narrowed.

Flag's face turned a dangerous shade of crimson and it looked like he was ready to sputter and spit but he managed to speak. "How dare you! I don't have to show either of you identification."

"That's not true," I chimed in. "Department policy clearly states that all officers must identify themselves to any civilian who asks."

Crunch cleared his throat. "Ahem. Dr. Jones, as your attorney, I must advise you to exercise your right to remain silent."

I nodded my head and made a zipping motion over my lips.

"I don't have to put up with this from either of you. I'll have you both dragged out at the station," Flag growled.

Shrill made a clicking sound and shook her head. "That would be a severe violation of our client's civil rights as well as our own, not to mention local laws and departmental policies. You simply cannot throw attorneys out for defending their client."

"Not to mention the fact that I don't think you have enough officers in the building to manage it," Crunch added with a grin that showed off his rather impressive incisors.

"You're big, but we're the NYPD. We'd take you down," Flag promised.

"Perhaps, but it was not my physical form I was referring to but my wife."

Flag squinted his eyes at Crunch and then back at Shrill. "You're married to this… this walking cellphone?"

Crunch gave Flag a bigger grin which opened his mouth wide enough that he showed all his teeth and this time let his lower incisors pop out of his mouth and up over his lips. They were each longer than most fingers. Flag swallowed loudly as his pupils dilated. The action had had its intended effect. Flag struggled to not tremble as sweat rolled down his face.

"Oh yes. Very happily for over two years now. The happiest years of my life, in fact."

Shrill's eyes orbs glowed on her faceplate and transformed into red hearts that were joined by a luminous line indicating a smile. "Mine as well, but we are not here to discuss our deliriously happy marriage with you but why you would think Mary Sue Jones kidnapped anybody."

Flag open the folder in front of him, pulled out an 8 x 10 photo, and slammed it down in front of me. "This is why."

The picture showed me talking to the Leviticus twins in the Bikini Tower lobby after they broke in. I suppose I was fortunate that they didn't get one of Sherman holding them off the ground by the scruffs of their shirts.

"Reverend and Mrs. Leviticus had reported their children missing over a week ago and spotted this picture on a news website which shows their missing 16-year-old son and daughter with your client. They have both sworn out an affidavit stating that Bikini Jones did not have permission to be with either of their children. And since she is seen clearly with them both, I think we have all the evidence we need." Flag smiled. "And while I may not be able to legally throw you out of the building, I can tell you to leave because the arrest has already been made and Bikini Jones will go before the judge for arraignment first thing in the morning. You can argue your bogus defense then."

"That seems an undue hardship for our client as she is unable to leave the jail on bail until she's been arraigned. As there is still time left in the court schedule for the day, not to mention night court, we request for her to be arraigned before the morning," Shrill said.

Flag leaned back in his chair and folded his hands over his slightly protruding belly. "Normally, I'd agree with you, but Bikini

Jones is a special case. As I'm sure you both well know, she has a great many enemies who might use this arrest as a chance to attack her. This would put not only your client in danger but anybody else in the vicinity of the courthouse. We have to arrange for an extra security detail to make sure that doesn't happen. Unfortunately, that will not be possible until the morning. I'm afraid your client is going to be spending the evening in the special wing at Rikers Island."

"Why is that? Mary Sue Jones has no unusual abilities or powers other than troubles wearing other types of clothing that one type of bathing suit," Crunch said. "Putting her in with extra-powered inmates places her in danger."

"Nonsense. Bikini Jones helped put in many of those inmates in there."

"Which is another reason why she should not be placed with those inmates who may want revenge. She would be practically defenseless. At least place her in protective custody away from the rest of the inmates," Shrill said.

"That won't be necessary. Our COs are the finest in the world and will make sure she's okay."

"Your logic for her imprisonment does not match up with your logic for her arraignment. On the one hand, you state that she's putting those around her in danger because she *might* be attacked by enemies yet you're putting her in jail with many actual, extra-powered enemies where she *will* likely be attacked."

"I don't see it that way and someone with the skillset of Bikini Jones hardly needs protective custody. Now leave so we can transfer her to Rikers Island." Flag stood.

Crunch also stood and towered over NYC's top cop. "Not so fast, Chief. Dr. Jones has not yet had the chance to speak to her attorneys in private, a right guaranteed to her by law. You will only be able to ship her to Rikers after she's met with us."

"Fine, but there are standards for the length of time a client under arrest can meet with her attorneys so don't think you can run out the clock until eight AM tomorrow. Feel free to use this room."

"I think not, especially with the built-in recording devices, microphones, and two-way glass," Shrill said.

Flag glared. "Are you implying that the NYPD would break the law to listen in on a confidential attorney-client conference?"

That was exactly what the mechanical attorney was doing, but it wasn't exactly prudent to admit it.

"Shrill said nothing of the sort," Crunch said. "Why, is that something you regularly do?"

Flag scowled. "Take Jones to an attorney room."

As two officers escorted me out, Flag gloated and smirked.

20

It wasn't my first time in jail, but it was my first time in Rikers, at least as an inmate.

Believe me, it's much more pleasant as a visitor. Shrill and Crunch did their best to get me into the general population where most people awaiting trial go, instead of Cell Block P (for powered of course). But the Chief just had too much pull. The problem was his using it to this degree made no sense. Flag had never liked me, but this made it seem like he was out to get me and abusing his power to do it, something any good cop avoids doing as a rule.

He had to know those kids were runaways, not kidnap victims, so why go through all this just to make sure I spent a night in Rikers?

I got there just before dinner and was last in the chow line. Not knowing who was cooking the food made me more than a little unwilling to even have a taste.

I took my tray to the far end of the mess hall and sat at an empty table by myself. I figured I could avoid trouble for one night.

It turns out that, like always, trouble came looking for me, this time in the guise of the Twister Sisters, a set of triplets whose father was allegedly the Northwind. Each had control over air and could make a one or two-story tornado. By working together and joining their hands in a circle, the triplets could create a tornado that would put the one that took Dorothy to Oz to shame.

Their life of crime started after they used their powers to kill their ex-boyfriend. Yes, all three of them were dating the same man but none of them knew it at the time. When they found out they used their powers to kill him and destroy half of their hometown before going on a bank robbing spree.

That's the part about supervillains that doesn't make much sense to me. They had superpowers. With some work, they could've learned to control the airstream and shift clouds to areas that had droughts and charge for it. A reasonable fee mind you, not extortion. It's legal and over the long-term would have made a lot more money than robbing banks.

They hit a bank where I was applying for a loan. Long story

short, I beat them and they ended up here. Judging from the way they slammed their trays down and then loomed over me, they hadn't forgiven or forgotten.

"Well if it isn't our arch-enemy, delivered to us on a platter."

They were hardly my arch enemies. I looked up and smiled, holding my tray as it was the only weapon I was likely to get.

"Esther, Hester, Lester."

Their mother wanted their names all to rhyme but the ultrasound only showed twins. Their stepfather chose the third name before his wife woke up from the anesthesia. They were identical except for the dyed hair–Esther was a blonde, Hester was a redhead, and Lester was blue-haired. Esther had been the one who'd spoken. "How's life in the big house treating you?"

"Lousy." Esther pointed to two ankle bracelets and a pair of wrist bracelets. Each one was a power inhibitor and worked independently of the others. Quadruple redundancy is not a bad idea when dealing with superpowered bad guys. If they managed to remove one, it wouldn't give them their powers back, but send an electric shock to the other three and an alarm to the guards. Basically, with the inhibitors, they were three ordinary women.

That didn't by any means imply they would be easy to take in a fight as it looked like all three of them had been spending most of their time using weights in the yard.

"That's too bad but you will be out of here in five years with good behavior. Doing something stupid to me would only add time to your sentences and let the other inmates watch me kick your butts."

"Last time you got lucky because we were soft and didn't know how to fight," Hester said, flexing her arms and showing off some impressive muscle bulk.

"We know how now and there are three of us and you're all alone," Lester said, pounding her right fist in her left palm. I was about a breath away from jumping up and smashing Esther's face with my tray while kicking out Hester's knee, then spinning to smash in Lester's nose with my elbow when a shadow fell over all four of us.

"Bikini Jones is not alone." I looked up to see Matoka smiling and showing off her many sharp teeth, looking surprisingly sharp in her orange prison jumpsuit. The shark woman put down her tray on the table. "And unlike you air-breathing sissies, I don't have any power dampening clamps on me."

That much was true. The dampeners worked on energy-based powers—mutations, magic, and the like. It didn't do anything to lessen physical strength.

The Twister Sisters went pale, held their hands up in front of them, and stepped back.

"We don't want no trouble with you, Matoka," Esther said.

"We surely don't," Hester said.

"We'll take our trays and go," Lester said.

"No. They barely feed me here." The shark woman's tray was twice as long and wide as the ones we humans had and the food was piled at least two feet high. "Leave them."

I could see Esther and Hester straining against the dampeners, trying to summon even a breeze but it wasn't working. Lester grabbed her two sisters by the backs of their orange scrubs and pulled them away.

Matoka sat down and dumped the contents of all three Twister Sisters trays into her mouth in rapid succession. The food was swallowed in one gulp.

I smiled at the shark woman. "I appreciate the help."

"It is a trifling gesture, a tiny gift to the savior of the shark people."

"Still, it saved me from a fight I didn't want to have." I'm trained in many fighting styles and rather good at controlled violence, but like the Clown Ninja Monks of Newark taught me, the best fight is one you never have. The second best involves cream pies, at least one banana peel, and killer punchlines.

"So why are you here in jail? Have the surface people turned against you?"

"Just one guy abusing his power." I gave her the rundown of what happened. "I'm hoping it'll be all sorted out tomorrow. Or if it isn't, then hopefully I'll at least make bail."

"Stay close to me. I'll make sure no one bothers you. We don't get to use the yard until after dinner as they won't let us mingle with gen pop or the powered male prisoners. Perhaps you can join me in a game of one-on-one basketball. It's my new favorite game. I can slam dunk without my feet even leaving the ground."

I didn't doubt it. "That sounds like it might be fun."

21

Igot more stares in the yard than I did in the mess hall. Genuine hate shone from many of the faces, most of which decided to glare from a safe distance once they noticed Matoka standing next to me.

Of course, there's always someone that insists on being the exception to the rule. Or two someones in this case.

It turns out superpowered prisoners join together in groups and gangs, the same as the ones without abilities. The two beautiful and statuesque blond women who approached me were apparently joined at the hip. It wasn't a surprise as they shared similar hateful beliefs on racial purity and extinguishing anyone who didn't share their Aryan heritage.

Annie Bellum and Blitz Meg were each recipients of the fruits of scientific experiments designed to increase the strength, speed, and endurance of the human body. Although not created by the same mad scientists, they shared similar abilities—they were about ten times as strong as an average person and three times as fast. I was the one who put each of them in here. The pair were a hate match, instantly bonding over their disdain for what they considered "the lesser peoples."

"I hope said your prayers and your goodbyes," Annie Bellum whispered as she cracked her knuckles.

"We got paid a lot of money to make sure you don't leave here alive," said Blitz Meg, looking at me like I was a hamburger and she was someone coming off a week-long fast.

I had to admit being more than a little perplexed. "Chief Flag put a hit on me?"

Blitz Meg spat on the ground. "We don't work for pigs."

"So then who put a hit on me?"

In an exaggerated drawl, Annie Bellum said, "Wouldn't you like to know?"

"It's pretty clear we've already established that."

"You know why we're not going to tell you? It's the same reason we took the hit. Look at you. You're the perfect Aryan female and yet you betray the master race time and time again helping mud people and lesser races and even…" Blitz Meg motioned with her hand towards Matoka. "… inhuman monstrosities. That is your sin, committed over and over again without remorse. It is unforgivable," the Nazi said.

Blitz Meg circled to one side of me and Annie Bellum moved to the other. A smart move as it would be harder to defend myself from attacks from opposite sides, at least if they timed their attack properly. Annie Bellum was a bit of a slacker in the education department but the Nazi had made a thorough study of tactics. One was a leader, the other a follower.

"Can't we all just get along?" I said.

"No, we can't." And with that, the Nazi came at me from my right, and the Confederate a second later from my left. I moved to defend myself against Blitz Meg first, but Matoka jumped between us. I didn't have time to warn her about how strong the Nazi was because Annie Bellum was still coming at me. I turned a moment too late to face off against the Confederate as she swung a fist right at my midsection.

I managed to get both forearms in front of me, not so much to block but to the cushion the blow. The force of the impact lifted me off the ground and tossed me a good ten feet. I barely managed to forget the pain long enough to manage a backward flip and land on my feet. It's one of the reasons I trained so hard. At a time like this, motor memory will save your life.

The Nazi's blow had moved the shark woman back about three feet. The faces of the Mano are more challenging to read than those of humans but I swear her expression was a mix of surprise and pleasure. The two of them charged each other as the Confederate leapt at me. I leapfrogged over her and planted my heel in the back of her neck while doing it.

Meanwhile, Matoka sidestepped the Nazis' next blow and leaned forward with open jaws. Two Aryan escapees from the lab were durable, but not invulnerable. The blond Nazi dove fast enough to avoid having her head bitten off but lost most of her hair to the shark woman's bite.

"No killing," I said.

"Something this hateful deserves to be put out of this world," Matoka shouted.

I didn't argue her point. "But if you do it here, they'll have all the evidence they need to lock you away." I motioned to cameras with my chin and noticed COs along the guardrail aiming rifles our way. I had no way of knowing if the same people who paid the hateful duo to kill me also paid any of the guards to kill them to keep them from talking. Or us if they failed.

I needed to end this.

The Confederate got up and cracked her neck as if to show me my blow hadn't bothered her. When she rushed me again, I was ready. I placed two fingers behind her ear and spun her in a circle, flipping her onto her back. I stomped my heel on her solar plexus, pivoted, and kicked her kneecap inwards to dislocate it.

She might be ten times as strong and three times as fast but her patella still worked the same way as a non-powered one. Knocking it out of joint meant she wasn't going to be able to stand, at least for the moment. Plus the pain would distract her while I spun again and rammed three fingers up into her brachial plexus through her sweaty and thoroughly unpleasant armpit. I maneuvered between her super-dense muscle to hit the nerves. She wouldn't be using that arm for a couple of hours.

Meanwhile across the yard, Blitz Meg wasn't smirking anymore. People used to being the strongest person in the room often couldn't figure out how to react when dealing with an opponent who out-muscled them.

The Nazi jumped on the shark woman's shoulders and tried to choke her out with a scissor kick, but her legs weren't long enough. Matoka just threw herself back onto the concrete, using the Nazi to cushion her impact.

I was on my way to help the shark woman end her fight quicker when I noticed red dots appear on her, then looked down and saw one on my chest. It was more than a little disturbing that neither of the racist duo was lit up by laser sites. It gave weight to my idea that one or more of the guards might have been paid to help kill us as well.

"Matoka, don't move. The guards have you in their sights."

The shark woman ignored me and turned to stare at the guards on the catwalk. "I doubt the bullets are going to do more than annoy me."

The shark woman's mutated form sported extremely dense

muscle, but that was a far cry from being bulletproof. It was the bad kind of interesting that rifles were in use when the guards for the powered cell block had weapons available that were much more effective and far less lethal.

I slowly raised my hands over my head in the universal gesture of "I give up." Annie Bellum hopped onto her good leg toward me and Blitz Meg leapt off the ground at my midsection.

Moving to defend myself would give a corrupt guard a reason to shoot me but doing nothing ended with me being killed by the super-strong racists.

I had to try to manage both. Without dropping my arms, I twisted to avoid the Nazi human torpedo but stopped short as a firehose-sized stream passed on either side of me. The streams weren't water.

They were made of worms.

That's it. This was how I was going to die. The Queen of Worms was going to have her revenge.

There are powers in this universe far greater than anything on Earth. And there are things from outside this universe that make those things look like gnats.

My Uncle Cthulhu was one of them. The Queen of Worms was another.

It started when a bullied and angry teenage boy got a hold of part of a page from the Necronomicon and summoned something from one of the dark universes. It wasn't done in ancient ruins or a dark temple. The boy brought an elder darkness into our universe in his garage near a refrigerator in which his stepfather—who was one of the primary reasons he was so hurt and angry—kept the bait he used for fishing.

Most things from the dark universes tend to manifest with many limbs, which are often seen by the human mind as tentacles. Unless they have a major power source available—the stars in special alignment, a virgin sacrifice, or some such—they can't exist in our world for very long. "Long" being a relative term as it could still be enough time to destroy a city and millions of lives. Because of this, the dark things will take the form of nearby living things and claim any convenient flesh for their own in order to anchor them to our universe. The angry boy was dumb enough to summon a creature from the darkness but smart enough to stand inside a protective circle, so the unspeakable horror he summoned could not wear his form so it went for the next closest thing—the worms.

To make a long story short, the live bait got loose, joined with more worms, and got bigger. At one point, the Queen was several stories tall.

To continue with the theme of making a long story short, I stopped but didn't destroy her, partly because doing so would have involved sacrificing the lives of a few hundred people and partly because the Queen of Worms had saved a life instead of taking one. I managed to get a spell slapped on her to keep her human-sized so she could stand trial. The Queen of Worms ended up here at Rikers as opposed to a more traditional penitentiary as they had the means to keep her contained. Although she was supposed to be fitted with mystically enhanced power dampeners which did not appear to be working.

It took me a moment to realize not only were my lungs not filling up with worms, but none had even touched my skin. A pivot of my head revealed that the racist duo were not so fortunate. Swarms of worms had cocooned and then pinned them to the ground. They struggled against the squirming mass for a minute, then stopped moving.

Dammit. I know it's tactically stupid, but I fight hard not to kill anybody, and I do mean anybody. Nobody died on my watch if I could help it.

Racing to Annie Bellum, the closest of the two, I used my hands to scoop worms away from her mouth and nose. As I struggled, a herd of creepies crawled along the concrete and merged into something roughly human-shaped but made of nothing but worms and two glowing eyes.

"Let your mind rest easy, Bikini Jones. These two hateful humans still live." The pulsating person-shaped swarm of invertebrates now sported a black hooded and ragged cloak that covered an orange prison jumpsuit. The worm swarm turned to look first at me and then at the shark woman before her focus took in the little red dots of light. "But it seems you may not have that luxury." The Queen of Worm's arms shot out and formed a large enough mass as to block both me and the shark woman from the sights of those with the rifles, preventing a clear shot.

A hole appeared where a mouth should be, followed by the

echoes of a voice so deep it shook my very skeleton and the entire prison.

"If any of you pathetic, mortal morsels act to harm either of these women, you will not enjoy another second before you follow them into the darkness of oblivion."

The wall of worms dropped and the red dots were gone. The two guards pointed their rifles downward.

"Thank you, Queen of Worms, but why help me?"

"When you defeated me, you could've destroyed me or sent me back to my dark dimension. Although here I am a great power, there I am an extremely minor one. The stink and light of life would mark me as having escaped and returned. Those far greater than me would have devoured my essence, my torture lasting an eternity. It was because of your mercy, a trait I'd never even imagined existed before arriving on Earth, that I allowed myself to be tried and imprisoned. To be honest, the mystic wards here are pathetic. I could leave any time. When you arrived, I thought it appropriate to protect the one that protected me."

We were surrounded by COs who were simultaneously furious, frightened, and confused. They realized they had no way to control the creature of elder darkness and therefore no way to make any of us do anything.

The Queen of Worm's arms suddenly snapped and contracted back to human-sized limbs. She pointed one arm at the worm-encased racists and their cocoons flew back into her body.

Turning to the highest-ranking CO, the Queen glared at him. The man took a step back. Mortals do not do well looking into what passed for eyes in something that had the power to devour their souls then swallow the world around them as a chaser.

"You may take the hateful ones away. I will converse with Bikini Jones. The three of us will return to our cells with no punishment once we are done speaking."

The CO in charge pulled out a high-powered Taser that was souped up enough to work on the empowered. He pressed a button so sparks surged from the business end.

"Convict, this is my house. You do not tell me what to do in my house. The three of you will lie down on the ground and..."

The guard didn't get a chance to finish his sentence because the Queen of Worm's arm shot out again and grabbed hold of the weapon, which he then fired at full strength.

Nothing happened. Not even one worm in her form so much as twitched, but they began devouring plastic and metal until the weapon was gone.

The tiny little worms suddenly had open hungry maws that hummed and hissed, millimeters from the CO's hand.

"This may be *your* house but if I so will it, this could be *my* world. I've already told you that we three will return to our cells. One more threat from you and I will rescind that offer."

Her hands sprouted tentacle shapes made from writing worms. A few other guards stepped forward with their weapons at the ready and the rest of her body produced more tentacles.

"The only reason I do not devour your soul and those of your fellows is because of the goodwill this woman has generated with me. Guard Jackson, do you take responsibility for angering the Queen of Worms? Are you willing to shoulder the guilt and shame for you and your fellow guards never returning to your spouses and offspring again? Do you wish your legacy, now and forever, to be known as the man who was too stubborn and dumb to allow all to live because, rest assured, on my way out, I will tear down this dwelling of trapped forms making sure that those above you on your food chain know the death and devastation was entirely your fault. Now you have a decision to make."

I stepped forward and smiled. "Sir, I recommend you listen to her. Matoka and I were only defending ourselves and the Queen of Worms in turn was only defending us. I also agree that we will return to our cells when this is done. Do you really want to escalate this simple discussion to a fight that the human race has no hope of winning?"

The corrections officer was trembling but didn't want to back down. "You stopped her once. You could stop her again."

"I'm a prisoner here and you and your guards did nothing to stop a public attempt on my life and you expect me to help you?" I would of course, but most people wouldn't and assumed others thought like they did. "Besides when I fought her before, I had preparations in place. I have nothing of the sort with me right now. You and your correction officers are it. Is it worth you and all your people here dying to prevent a conversation?"

The CO inhaled and nodded. "Let's go."

One of the guards who had had a rifle pointed at us gritted his teeth. "Fine, but Wormy, as soon as you're back in your cell, we're reattaching your dampening belt and bracelets."

The writhing flesh of the Queen's abdomen parted to reveal a shiny dampening belt, followed by her wrists and ankles doing the same.

"Why would you need to replace something that I never took off?"

I didn't think the guards could turn any paler, but they did. Most struggled not to run out of the yard. One was muttering about retiring.

22

"You have my attention. What's so important?"

The Queen of Worms made a wet raspy sound that was her equivalent of a sigh.

"Because of my nature, I am still connected to the realm of primordial darkness that spawned me. Something is trying very hard to cross over from my shadowy home. Soon, the planets and stars will align, thinning the wall between your universe and mine and it will arrive. I am frightened."

"Why would you be frightened of another elder thing?" I asked.

"Just like there is no mercy in the darkness, there is also no friendship, although there can be alliances. What is scratching at the door to your world is more powerful than I am. To use your companion's physiology as an example, I am a tiger shark. It is a great white, the child of a megalodon." A giant dinosaur-era shark that makes the great white look like a flounder.

"What is the thing's name?" I said.

"Our names are not meant for human tongues but this one has not yet been named because its parent is sleeping beneath the depths of your ocean."

"Cthulhu?" I doubted what was coming through would be as kind as my cousin.

The mass of worms shook what passed for her head. "Dagon."

Which just happened to be the so-called god The Church of the Majestic Deep worshiped.

"That would explain the uneasiness and what I felt lurking in the water. This thing is not going to arrive on land but in our river!" Matoka said.

"The shark woman is right which is why I am preparing to flee. Bikini, I hereby offer to take you with me," the Queen of Worms said.

That was unexpected as well as oddly touching. It's not often a thing of elder darkness shows either honor or compassion.

"Many thanks for your gracious and generous offer, Queen of Worms, but I cannot go. I have to try to stop the incursion."

Another moist sucking sound escaped the Queen's mass

of wriggling flesh. "A pity. You are one of the few mortals I find tolerable."

"Can you take my people with you instead?" Matoka asked.

The moist and meaty mass of squirminess moved what passed for a head side to side. "I will not. You and your kin by your nature are bound to the water as will be this invading darkness. Your presence would expose me to discovery."

The shark woman growled. "Such great cowardice..."

I risked losing my hand by reaching up and placing it near the shark woman's mouth.

"Matoka, hush please." The Queen of Worm could devour her faster than a school of Jupiterian piranha. "Queen of Worms, please don't escape just yet. I might be able to stop this from happening."

The writhing collective of oblong creatures made a sucking sound from beneath the hood of her black cloak that brought to mind a boot being pulled out of thick mud and a thousand bodies vibrating together. "There is not much chance of you succeeding."

"You may be surprised," I said. "If you escape, the authorities will try to recapture you and the results would be unfortunate."

"No number of mortals could capture me if I did not allow it. You were lucky with the spell when we first clashed but that was a temporary measure. I will not be taken the same way again. Any mortals who dare come after me will perish."

"Which is exactly my point. You are an ageless being. The rest of your sentence will pass in what would be a day for the rest of us. When that happens, they will let you go and no one will be hunting you."

Her chin rose and dipped as if invisible fingers were stroking the worms there. "I expected a threat, not a plea to save inconsequential lives. Very well. I will stay for now. But should you fail, you and your ilk as well as the invading darkness will never see me again."

I didn't point out that if I didn't stop it that in all likelihood I would never see anything again.

There was something I suspected but wanted to confirm my suspicions. "Do you know who was trying to summon the darkness to this realm?"

The glowing eyes rolled back so far in her head that they disappeared for a moment before popping back into place. "I can feel the page of the Necronomicon that outlines the ritual. I know where it is and who has it. After all, worms are everywhere in this world and what they know, I know." That was something I didn't know. "It is the same man who leads the worship of the hateful sea elder and sent the head of your city's legions of law—" Translation, Reverend Leviticus and Chief Flag. "—to eliminate you from the equation so you wouldn't interfere with something that can only happen in your city. Otherwise, they would undoubtedly have retreated to some deserted island or wasteland."

"If I can get a hold of that page and destroy it..."

"Very unlikely. This close to the alignment, that page will take on sentience that will drive it to do whatever is possible to make the intrusion of darkness become reality. With the only two days to go, I doubt any destruction born of mortal means will harm that page."

"If I can't destroy it, there still might be other options." Seal it in cement, launch it into space, or have a toddler spill their sippy cup of grape juice on it.

The worms beneath the dark cloak vibrated like the wings of a hummingbird. "You've given me another reason to stay in this place. A chance to see if you will destroy this greater darkness. If you succeed, you will save my existence and I will again be indebted to you."

Thousands of pieces of undulating worm flesh reached out in imitation of an arm and a single worm broke apart from the mass and crawled onto the tip of her index finger. "Bikini Jones, I ask of you a boon. Take this part of me and keep it on your person, so I may observe what happens."

Great. The Queen of Worms wanted me to be her personal reality show.

The world of magic is big on tit for tat. "If I grant you this boon, what am I offered in return?"

More sucking and vibrating noises. "Oh, how you amuse me, Bikini Jones. Again, instead of making a demand, you make a request. Had you tried to command me or refused, I would have embedded my flesh in your own, but since you showed the proper respect, I shall do the same. I offer you my assistance in your quest through the part of me I offer to you, you may ask for my help a single time. So long as it would not ensure my destruction, I shall grant it. Do we have an agreement?"

"We do." I took the worm from her finger. Where to put it?

"Would it offend you if I used it to bind my hair?"

It wasn't that I wanted a worm in my hair but it seemed a better place than on my bare skin.

"It is acceptable," The Queen of Worms said. "Come. We should return to our cells before the guard of this place of imprisonment have their circulatory system pumps explode."

The bottom of the worm mass—which was one solid form that did not bother to pretend any imitation of legs–slithered back toward the door.

Matoka and I followed behind. The shark woman leaned over to whisper in my ear.

"You have the most interesting friends."

23

"Your Honor, I put forth that the prosecution has not made their case and, as per the motion I filed earlier, that this is harassment of my client on the deepest and most heinous level," Crunch said, able to look at the judge on the bench directly in the eyes.

"Your Honor, this is the arraignment, not the trial. I object to this. The defendant should just enter a plea so we can move on to bail," said the ADA.

"Mr. Werner, from where I sit your case is on shaky ground. I'm going to review the defense's motion."

My legal team was both upset and happy that we got Judge Olson. Upset because he was a no-nonsense type who tended to favor the DA's office in cases that had any doubt. Happy because he was such a curmudgeon and an absolute stickler for the letter of the law that both of my attorneys doubted highly that anyone could've bribed him successfully as they did Chief Flag or the two corrections officers.

"The accusation behind these charges is that the defendant Mary Sue Jones kidnapped Loraine and Isaac Leviticus from their home. Other than affidavits from the parents, I've seen no evidence that these teenagers were taken against their will or coerced in any way," Crunch said.

The ADA stood up defiantly. "Your Honor, the children's father is a very prominent member of the community as such as his integrity is above…"

The judge cut the ADA off. "How much money the father donated to your boss's campaign doesn't excuse him from scrutiny in my courtroom," Judge Olsen said.

"Your honor, we have provided affidavits from both of the *allegedly* kidnapped teenagers that they ran away and went to Ms. Jones for help," Shrill said.

"A private citizen doesn't have the right to help minors not go home to their parents and this admission should only add more weight to the kidnapping charges," Werner said.

"As questionable as that statement may be, the Bikini Foundation, which is owned by the defendant, runs several shelters including one for runaways. These teenagers are staying in one of these shelters. It is certified by New York State's Division of Shelter Oversight and Compliance and thus is recognized by the State of New York so that it may take in unaccompanied minors," Shrill said.

"So if Dr. Mary Sue Jones is being charged with something the State of New York has certified her charity to do, this could set a precedent where upset parents can charge those who run shelters with kidnapping, I suspect that all shelters will either choose to close or refuse to take in children, which means homeless children will have no place to go and will be exposed to dangers that shelters protect them from," Crunch said. "The DA's office appears to be allowing a wealthy and influential religious leader to set its policy. Another dangerous precedent. We can also show a pattern of harassment of Dr. Jones by the mother of these teens, of which these false charges are the culmination."

ADA Werner stood in a huff. I suspected his comments might take more than a minute and a huff. "Your Honor, the only one involved her who is abusing her power and privilege is the defendant. Does she run shelters that take in runaways? I suppose that might be true. That does not give her the right to go out and bring children into the shelter by force."

"Objection, your Honor. The prosecution has no evidence of coercion of any kind being used let alone force," Shrill said, looking over at me. This would be the perfect point for her to insert the Chief's abuse during my arrest. We would deal with that, but I didn't want that to be part of why this case got thrown out of court. Then people would have doubts about my guilt or innocence if I got off on a technicality.

I kept silent, so she did as well.

The judge glared at ADA Warner. "I'm inclined to believe the defense on this. The only evidence you appear to have is the testimony of two parents, one of whom has demonstrated negative behavior toward the defendant. As the prosecution has no other witnesses, the affidavits of the two minors would seem to negate those of the parents. This seems like more of a matter for family court than criminal. I'm dismissing all charges against the defendant."

The ADA's face went pale I had a good idea why. My hacker squad dug up a few things indicating that Warner was accepting financial remuneration as part of this railroad job.

I high-fived my attorneys. Crunch was very gentle as his palm dwarfed mine. Despite having a metal limb, Shrill had enough motor control so that we high-fived without any pain or damage to my hand.

"*Now* do we get to reveal what the bad guys did?" Shrill asked.

I couldn't stop myself from enjoying a wicked grin. "Oh yes."

Shrills glowing eyes shifted on her faceplate from a pleasant sky-blue to an angry crimson and a line formed a wicked grin of her own.

24

We walked out of the courthouse into a mob of reporters shouting questions like firecrackers going off.

"After going through this, are you going to close shelters?"

"Bikini, did you get that black eye and bruises on your face from resisting arrest?"

All it took was Crunch to raise one huge hand in front of them for everyone to fall silent.

"Although her innocence was never in doubt, we are incredibly pleased with the court for finding that there was not a shred of evidence to show that Bikini Jones did anything wrong and is innocent of all charges." The rapid-fire questions began again.

Crunch raised his hand and quiet came again. "However, the same cannot be said for those involved in this sham. And as for the brutal damage to Dr. Bikini Jones' face, that was done while she was *not* resisting arrest." The ogre turned to his android wife. A beam of light radiated out of her forehead and showed a hologram of what the Chief had done to me. It showed me offering no resistance to the arrest and him grabbing me by the hair and slamming my face down onto my desk.

"As you can see, NYC Police Chief Arnold Flag abused his office by pursuing a personal vendetta against my client. Chief Flag unlawfully attacked and injured her while she was handcuffed and helpless for no other reason other than he could. Although that is not exactly true." Crunch held up a stack of papers in his hand. "We found evidence that Police Chief Arnold Flag took half a million dollars in crypto-currency as a bribe from Reverend Leviticus of the Church of the Majestic Deep immediately prior to instituting this sham of an arrest. We can also prove that ADA Warner who brought the charges against Bikini Jones similarly took two hundred thousand dollars in crypto-currency from Reverend Leviticus. These two men sold their honor and their vows to uphold the laws of the City of New York to the highest bidder and tried to put an innocent woman in jail. Worse, Arnold Flag plotted to have Bikini Jones murdered by arranging for her to go to the extra-powered ward at Rikers Island, despite the fact that my client has no enhanced abilities or powers. While she was falsely imprisoned, two convicts made an attempt on her life and two guards allowed it to happen."

Our hackers got into the Rikers Island security feed and downloaded the footage of me in the courtyard being attacked and the two guards training lethal weapons on me instead of the extra-powered racists trying to kill me. Shrill projected an edit of what happened in her hologram.

"We can show transfer of crypto-currency worth twenty-five thousand dollars to each of these corrections officers and fifty thousand to each convict. We hereby demand that Chief Flag, ADA Warner, and Corrections Officers Samuel Page and Harold White be suspended from their positions immediately and that they be investigated for bribery, false imprisonment and arrest, and attempted murder. We will make the recordings and other evidence that we have available to the press. Copies are currently en route to the DA's office and the New York State Attorney General."

Shrill turned off the hologram display and spoke up. "If you'll excuse us, our client has had a very traumatic few days, and we're going to get her back to Bikini Tower so she can rest and recuperate."

Crunch cleared a path simply by walking through the crowd of reporters while Shrill wrapped an arm around my shoulder and escorted me toward a waiting town car.

Every step was peppered by more questions from reporters.

"Will you be suing the city and all those involved?"

"Will you be suing the Reverend Leviticus?"

"Will you be getting plastic surgery for your face? Will you be getting another boob job and more butt implants?"

I ignored them, but for the record, my only surgeries have been to repair injuries or to remove implanted technology or alien symbiotes.

As for suing Leviticus, I was more worried about how to stop him from summoning a creature of ancient darkness.

If the world survived the week, I'd worry about everything else then.

25

Leviticus wore a dark gray two-piece suit that was worth about five times what I paid for my first car. The material had gray-green highlights that matched the Reverend's scaly skin. After all, a cult of sea monsters can't have a human being in charge. The other Deep Ones would never listen.

The reverend sported a layer of darker green scales on top of his head where hair would be on a human. I suspected he had his scales trimmed precisely to look like a five-hundred-dollar haircut. He wore a pair of sunglasses which did a halfway effective job of covering up his yellow eyes. The sclera–the white part in humans–was a pale yellow, but the iris was a very vibrant, almost golden hue. His fingers were longer than a typical man's and ended in trimmed but sharp claws. In between each finger was a flap of skin that gave him webbed hands. It made everyday tasks a bit more awkward but really upped his swimming speed. He walked to his press conference podium with a swagger and stood—or rather posed—with the confidence of a movie star.

He got right to business.

"Bikini Jones is a fraud and a liar."

The words made me smile. Not because I was a fan of people speaking poorly about me but it meant that the Reverend Leviticus had taken the bait. And the amphibiman did look a bit like a fish.

It is usually considered poor business practice for someone to get up in front of a press conference and start by saying bad things and criminal acts were performed by someone who can afford excellent lawyers, even if the speaker is wealthy enough to afford good lawyers of their own. Under normal circumstances, there would be lawsuits for defamation of character and the like filed and counter-filed quickly.

Leviticus wasn't worried about being sued which made perfect sense from his point of view. After all, if everything went according to his plan–and he had no reason to think it wouldn't—tomorrow he would summon a creature of elder darkness, the son of the very elder god his cult worshiped. No doubt he assumed he'd have control of the eastern seaboard within a day or two, the rest of the country in a week. Since the current monetary system would be rendered meaningless, there was no reason for him to care about lawsuits.

But he still needed his plan to summon Dagon Junior to work.

Between now and the alinement of stars, he couldn't afford to be arrested. It would be difficult to smuggle his page from the Necronomicon into jail. True, he could swallow it, but the bad juju would likely either kill or possess him. Or both.

That meant he had to come out swinging against the only person who stood a chance of stopping him. And of course, that person happened to be me.

Having him shoot his mouth off at the press was all part of my plan. True it might be a little flimsy, but I'd had worse plans succeed. Then again, I've had better plans fail.

"The evidence against you looks pretty damning," a reporter said with a smile. The word damning in a headline about the Reverend would be something the press would have twisted fun with.

"Phony news. It's all fabricated, a campaign by Bikini Jones to discredit me. But with Dagon as my witness, it will not work. Enemies of my church may try to knock me down, but Dagon raises me back up."

"So you deny the allegations?" asked a reporter.

"Emphatically and with every fiber of my being."

The reporter nodded. "I'll put that down as a yes."

A woman reporter named Christina Goal spoke up. "What do you say to the charges leveled against The Church of the Majestic Deep that you only want to take people's money?"

What he would call donations. Leviticus might not be on the top three list of televangelists, but he was no slouch. His church took in over twenty-five million last year. Plus, he told his worshippers that Dagon wanted him to have an extra few million to buy a yacht and people gave it to him.

"And that it treats women not only as inferior but the property of the men in the church."

"Utter nonsense. Like many other churches, we believe that the man is the head of the household and the wife—" Leviticus almost said wives but stopped himself before he finished the last syllable.

"—should honor, respect, and obey her husband in every way. If you going to come after me for that, you'll have to go after a lot of Christian, Jewish, and Muslim faiths as well."

"Unlike the other three faiths you mentioned, your God is not a creator but a destroyer."

"No more than Shiva. And what about Noah's flood or the destruction of Sodom and Gomorrah?"

"Traditionally worship of Dagon involves working towards the destruction or enslavement of the human race. Isn't that your church's ultimate goal?" asked Christina Goal, who was trying to pierce him with her glare.

"If you're asking me if I can control the intentions of a god, then I have to tell you no. We at The Church of the Majestic Deep do our best to honor both Dagon and the human race exactly as our god instructs us."

I stood off to the side, keeping a news van between me and Leviticus and his wife on the stage. The reporter Christina Goal was a friend of mine and hopefully was about to set me up for the win with her next question.

"So is it true that The Church of the Majestic Deep is a closed cult that will not allow outsiders to join?" Christina Goal asked.

Leviticus made a big show of laughing. "Nothing could be further from the truth. We welcome all truth seekers and the faithful to join our church."

"So what if I wanted to join your church right now? What would I have to do?" Christina asked.

"In our ministry, women are needed to bring forth the next generation, so all a woman needs to do to join our church is to ask," Leviticus said with a predatory leer toward Christina, a remarkably attractive woman. Sad to say it's hard to get on a major TV network if you're not.

His answer was my cue. I stepped out from behind the van and shouted to ensure I was heard. "I ask to be allowed to join The Church of the Majestic Deep."

The crowd of reporters spun to see who had made that offer and all the cameras turned towards me so for the benefit of those who would later be watching the evening news I repeated myself.

"I ask to be allowed to join The Church of the Majestic Deep."

The Reverend Leviticus was professional. Although the smile

dropped away from his face, he kept a stoic expression, unlike his wife who looked as if she wanted to come at me with a chainsaw.

"As I said we only take truth seekers and the faithful."

I walked through the crowd of reporters toward his stage. "My entire life has been spent seeking the truth and I am faithfully devoted to learning the secrets of the universe."

"You can't join us. You're just some shameless hussy who dresses like a harlot," Mrs. Leviticus screeched.

"For the last week, you've spent all your time attacking me personally and professionally for who and what I am. I come here to offer an olive branch in hopes that we can better get to know each other and end this hostility and you tell me no? So what you are really saying is your husband just lied about the very tenets of your religion to these people? Which means he was probably lying when he said he had nothing to do with the attempt on my life?"

In his religion, Leviticus was much like the Pope. If he said something, it was considered as coming from Dagon's own scaly lips.

The beauty of this is he had trapped himself. If he refused, I could demand his immediate arrest in front of reporters. We'd be viral by lunch and he'd be arrested by supper.

Now to play on his desire to stay out of jail for the next day. "You say you're innocent and did not bribe and plot to have me arrested and killed. Denying me the opportunity to seek the truth will only convince me you did it. I suppose I should go visit the mayor for a chat about why you aren't in custody. I believe they can hold you for seventy-two hours without even arresting you."

Which meant he'd be in custody until after the stars moved out of alignment again.

If my plan didn't work, I might have to fall back on that as Plan B.

"On the other hand, if what your say about your religion is true, perhaps I could be convinced you are also being falsely accused."

Not likely.

Leviticus paused, then his scaly face smiled. "My wife speaks from a place of passion instead of speaking Dagon's truth. We would welcome you to our fold, Bikini Jones." His smile ramped up and looked just the tiniest bit evil. "Provided you can follow what is demanded of postulants."

The Reverend looked at his prime wife and motioned with his chin toward a bag that was on the platform behind them. Mrs. Leviticus didn't bother to hide the evil in her grin as she reached down and pulled out a long-sleeved hooded robe that reached all the way to the ankles.

"We require postulants, both male and female, to wear these robes for the first year they spend in our church." His eyes twinkled and I half expected him to rub his hands together then tilt back his head and laugh maniacally. "If you would join us, you must put on the robe."

They'd undoubtedly seen the recording of me putting on the T-shirt at the protest outside Bikini Tower and what happened.

Without flinching I took the robe, lifted it over my head, and slid it down around me. My head ended up in the hood. It was made of a pink spandex blend and was extremely formfitting.

I didn't try to prolong it from disappearing and instead focused on making sure my new bikini was the color pink.

A moment later the robe was gone although the hood remained.

"I'm so sorry, Bikini Jones, but it appears you cannot fulfill the requirements of a postulant as you cannot wear the robe."

"So you're willing to violate the Americans with Disability Act by using that as an excuse to deny me entrance?"

Mrs. Leviticus turned red and shouted, "You have no disability! Other than being a whore!"

I ignored the whore comment. Also not sure why she would think that was a disability. "Not true. The Supreme Court has ruled that mystic curses and the like fall under the ADA." The case that did it was thanks to my parents. My high school principal didn't want to allow me back into school after Mrs. Doomhilda cursed me because bikinis violated the dress code. And it fed his uptight desire to impose his morality on other people. My parents hired a lawyer, sued, and helped set a legal precedent.

"I'll inform His Honor when I get to Gracie Mansion. Maybe I can get my lawyers to get an immediate spot on the court docket like we did for Voxamatik for your failure to make reasonable adjustments rising from my disability."

Leviticus was behind the toxic dumping to take out the shark people so he knew we managed that. I hoped he didn't realize there was no chance an ADA compliant would be considered urgent enough to get him called into court that quickly. I just needed him to believe he might get tied up in court when he needed to be summoning a dark entity.

The media could be manipulated into backing calls for his immediate arrest. Not to mention make him look bad. I suspected his ego couldn't take that hit, even if it wouldn't matter the day after tomorrow.

"Very well. Since your bikini at least matches the color of the robes and you are willing to wear the hood, we will make accommodations for you. Of course, you do realize that the first year as a postulant is very important to the women who join our church as they need to spend that time among the blessed to choose which of the faithful will become their husband." Translation, which Deep One would get to knock me up. "Are you willing to accept that?"

"I'm willing to consider that possibility if The Church of the Majestic Deep meets my spiritual needs." Which he and I both knew it wouldn't.

Leviticus slowly nodded, ignoring the death glare his prime wife was sending his way. "Very well." He turned to the throng of reporters. "Allow me to introduce all of you to the latest postulant member of The Church of the Majestic Deep, Bikini Jones." There was no applause, just a lot of shocked looks.

I didn't care. I needed to find the Necronomicon page and I had a better chance inside the Deep Compound than out.

26

We rode in the back of the limo with me sitting facing backward and the Reverend and Mrs. Leviticus opposite me.

Mrs. Leviticus looked like she had sucked on a bushel of lemons. The woman couldn't stop glaring at me, except when she turned her glare sideways on her husband who thought just because he was wearing sunglasses that we couldn't tell that he was leering at my cleavage.

"I don't know what you hope to accomplish with this farce, Miss Jones. Religion and faith are very serious matters and not to be taken lightly or mocked."

"I agree."

"I'm going to get my son back," he said.

"Our son," Mrs. Leviticus replied in a tone so cold it sent shivers up my spine. "And our daughter too."

Again, Reverend Leviticus assumed we couldn't see him rolling his eyes behind his sunglasses. "Of course. Our daughter too."

"Why all the sudden interest in your son?" Mrs. Leviticus somehow managed to increase the power levels on her glare so I amended my statement. "In your children. According to the twins, you've let them run away numerous times before and waited weeks before trying to find them. One time you didn't try for two months." I had my suspicions about why. As the firstborn and only son of the cult leader, Isaac was positioned to replace his father in a century. Deep Ones live a long time but don't believe the hype. They are far from immortal. Still, the son had value as an heir, if for no other reason than to shelter Leviticus from a rival assassinating him with the thought of taking over."

A daughter had no true value to him except perhaps to barter with an influential cult member as a wife.

"Being a parent is quite difficult yet immensely important. Something someone such as you his no inkling of," Mrs. Leviticus said from atop her high sea horse. Yeah, I had no kids and in this jerk's mind not being a mother somehow made me less of a woman.

"As Dagon's direct line to his faithful here on Earth, I am infallible in matters of faith."

Right. Dagon doesn't care about the little stuff and doubt he has much to relay. The rules are all Leviticus's.

"As a father, I am left to my own devices. My children are ungrateful brats. Their every material need has been met beyond most teens' wildest dreams but they see my power and the devotion of the faithful to me and it makes them jealous. And perhaps a little hurt that leading Dagon's faithful takes up so much of my time that there is less of it to spend with them. A certain amount of resentment is only to be expected. My children have gone well beyond what is acceptable."

"Acceptable to Dagon? Or to you? There are those among your faithful who feel that your son transforming as a teenager instead of in his mid-twenties or thirties is a sign of Dagon's favor. A favor he did not grant you. Perhaps *you* are the jealous one. Is that why both your children have described mental and physical abuse? Do you think by tormenting him the way you do, you'll keep him in line instead of him realizing that he could soon replace you as Dagon's chosen?"

The effortlessness at which the smile took over Leviticus's face told me all I needed to know. That was exactly right.

"Perhaps if you ever decide to leave the adventurer life behind, you might try your hand becoming a novelist with such an overactive imagination."

"I don't think that the bruises and scars on both of your children are the product of my or anyone's imagination. The shelter arranged for the children to have a full medical workup which revealed a host of old injuries on both of them. Those records will be entered into evidence for their emancipation trial."

"How dare you put such horrid thoughts into the minds of my babies! You're far more wicked than just your whore outfits make you seem, trying to break up a happy family for no good reason," Mrs. Leviticus said.

"Mental and physical abuse is a very good reason. And I think your version of happy differs greatly from mine."

Leviticus grinned. "Now we'll get to see how developed your claim of devotion to The Church of the Majestic Deep really is. Members must obey the head of the church in all things and I hereby command you to drop all your efforts, including legal ones, towards having my children emancipated from me."

"Us," corrected Mrs. Leviticus. The Reverend ignored her and focused all his attention for once on my face.

"Would you mind explaining your request from a theological perspective?" I asked.

"It's quite simple really. If your desire to join us is true, then you have to obey me and stop trying to break up my family. And if it's not, I get to put an end to this farce and kick you out of my limo. Either way, I get something I want."

"I have to say that I am truly amazed that someone who claims to be the head of a church can be ignorant of some of its most basic tenets. In this case, the third book of Dagon and the rules that govern women postulates. And I quote 'Because of the high burden that will be placed upon women they must be given a year and a day for discernment during which time they are permitted to not follow all the precepts of the church should they choose not to, for like Mother Hydra, they shall bear responsibility for the raising of the young.'" Mother Hydra is the dark consort of Dagon. "Thus, to give full meaning to their final vows to Dagon, they must be allowed to make up their own mind so there will be no regrets upon giving themselves body, mind, and soul to the church."

I watched the smile melt away from Leviticus's face and Mrs. Leviticus's face became a frightening shade of crimson.

"Women are forbidden from reading the holy books! You have committed blasphemy!"

"Not true. Women are allowed to read the Books of Dagon before taking their final vows to the church. As I have taken no such vow, I can read whatever I like without blaspheming." Fortunately, I'm a very fast reader.

"I am more concerned with where you acquired a copy of the complete books of Dagon as they are banned from outsiders and women believers. Did one of my children provide them to you?"

"Not at all. I trained with the Clown Ninja Monks of Newark. The monks have an extensive collection of religious literature saved and digitized. I simply borrowed the e-book versions from their library."

The only way I could describe Leviticus is that he glowered. "I see. I will have to pay the shadow clowns a visit and demand they permanently withdraw those holy books from their library."

"Good luck with that." The shadow clowns have dedicated their lives to the dichotomy of laughter and darkness and are proficient at both. The monks are among the deadliest fighters on the planet. Invading their monastery is akin to committing suicide. Sure, Deep Ones are stronger than humans, but not all the monks are human. And even a human monk would be more than a match for Leviticus and any dozen of his followers. "Should you be foolish enough to try, your son will be inheriting your mantle sooner than expected."

Mrs. Leviticus's fingernails had dug into the upholstery and I could hear Leviticus's teeth grind.

"As my researching the church could not possibly be misconstrued as having a bad intent, I choose to follow Dagon's guidance. I refuse your order with a quote from the Fourth Book of Dagon. 'Whatever you do for the protection of one of the children of Dagon—'" Fancy speak for Deep One. "'—is done to Dagon the father.' So my protecting one who has gone through his holy transformation is considered one of the most blessed acts a member of the church can perform. But you know this. Obviously, this was your way of testing me and I am so happy to have passed."

We all knew it was no such thing, but he confirmed my suspicion that he was recording this when he simply smiled and nodded his head.

The limo stopped and the driver got out and walked towards the back door.

"Are we not going to the Majestic Deep compound on the coast of Delaware?"

"If you are referring to the cloister, we will go there another time. For now, I have pending business in Manhattan to attend to."

While I'm not sure preparing to summon a creature of elder darkness counts as business, I played along.

"I'm quite proficient in matters of business. Perhaps I could be of assistance."

"I think not, Postulate Jones." The limo driver ran around and opened the door. "I leave you now to my wife's tender mercies so she can begin acclimating you into the church."

Reverend Leviticus got out of the car and marched off. We were on Battery Place, right next to the Battery, a park that overlooked the south end of Manhattan where the East River and the Hudson

River merged. It was a nice neighborhood but The Church of the Majestic Deep's teleservices made quite a bit of money, so I guess Leviticus could afford the real estate prices.

Mrs. Leviticus regained her composure and her enormous attitude.

"Postulate Jones, you will follow five paces behind me and we will begin your duties to the church. Follow me."

She stepped out and started walking. When I didn't instantly appear behind her, she turned back and began snapping her fingers like an entitled brat summoning wait staff. As a former waitress, I'd seen others spit in someone's food for being far less offensive.

"Don't dawdle. Get a move on."

I got out of the limo, bumping the driver, then followed her into a building with an awning that read *The Church of the Majestic Deep*.

Hopefully, I could slip off to search for the page of the Necronomicon. As this was Leviticus's stronghold in Manhattan, it only made sense that it would be here somewhere.

This kind of evil magic tried to protect itself. Anyone trying to find it would feel the urge to ignore going in any direction that would lead them to it. Of course, anyone with any experience simply turns that to their advantage by going in the opposite direction their gut tells them.

It would get more dangerous as I got closer as the dark magic could take over any living thing in the vicinity to attack me.

I was wearing a pair of simple gold studs that held a microphone and a camera, so I knew at least that there were people back at Bikini Tower monitoring me, including the mole woman Aditte who would get *The Brass Ring* airborne to come get me at a moment's notice.

Too bad that sometimes a moment is all it takes to lose your life.

27

I felt like I was suddenly Cinderella. There was no ball, no prince, no fairy godmother but there was someone filling the role of the evil stepmother who thought I was her servant girl. We were in a conference room that had been set up with rows and rows of folding chairs facing the front where there was a screen that could be used for presentations.

"First fold up all the chairs, put them on the cart, take them in the hallway, then scrub down the floors, walls, and ceiling. When I come back, I want them to shine so much I can see my face's reflection," Mrs. Leviticus said.

I looked around the place. "No problem on the floor, but you know the walls are sheetrock with matte paint and the ceilings are drop-down bumpy tiles. No amount of scrubbing is going to make those surfaces reflective," I said.

The first wife of the Cult of the Majestic Deep grinned but there was no joy in it, just malice. "I guess you're never going to be able to stop scrubbing then, are you? That is unless your faith falters and you no longer want to be a part of the church."

Instead of rolling my eyes, I just nodded my head. "I'll see what I can do so it doesn't look too bad."

Her grimace turned into a genuine smile. Something I said had made her happy. That didn't bode well.

"You're right, Postulant Bikini. This is hardly a task worthy of someone who's a true believer in Dagon."

She walked to a closet, opened it, and pulled out a canister vacuum cleaner. Mrs. Leviticus didn't offer it to me. Instead, she opened it up and reached inside the closet. Her hands emerged with several bags of cooking supplies including flour, salt, sugar, and breadcrumbs.

The prime wife tore each bag open and then dumped its contents into the vacuum. When it was full, she pointed the vacuum hose in front of her and switched the vacuum on.

The canister vacuum wasn't set to clean but blow. Mrs. Leviticus waved the nozzle end of the hose back and forth like she was imitating a fairy godmother with her wand as she walked around the conference room spraying every surface with the powdery mix.

When the vacuum was only blowing air, she turned it off. The place looked like a grimy winter wonderland. Mrs. Leviticus smiled at me. "Now there's a task more worthy of the legendary Bikini Jones."

I've been chained to sacrificial altars, subjected to mad scientist experiments, and thrown out of planes. I was even tied to train tracks. Twice. So my expression didn't change over a little housecleaning. It seemed to disappoint her.

I held up my hand for the vacuum cleaner, but she pulled it away and moved behind her back like she was hiding it from me.

"Surely the legendary Bikini Jones doesn't think she's going to simply use a vacuum to prove her faith."

Mrs. Leviticus reached into her pocket and pulled out a teaspoon and a toothbrush and held them out to me.

"These are your cleaning tools. You will not be permitted to sleep or eat into the job is complete."

I expected no less. Cults and other organizations that trafficked in brainwashing made sure they controlled all aspects of somebody's life. They give their members enough food to provide substance but no more. Perhaps they'd drug the food as it saved time. When they let me sleep, it would be for a brief time, with something playing in the background. Probably awful music or someone reciting selected scripture from the Books of Dagon. The idea being the person subjected to all that would be broken down so when they finally embraced the Reverend Leviticus and The Church of the Majestic Deep the return to more sleep and food would be since as a reward for their piety.

I've gone without sleep before and I'd taken several time-release capsules before I went to the press conference that would release a mix of nutrients and stimulants into my system over the next few days. Plus a few others that would provide hydration. I could probably last for a week before having to touch their food and at least a few days before I needed a nap.

As if to prove me right, Mrs. Leviticus started playing scriptures over the speakers. I employed meditative techniques the Clown Ninja Monks of Newark had taught me to help me focus through the propaganda.

I took the toothbrush and spoon out of her hand.

"I guess I better get started then." I pulled a large garbage can over by me and picked up the first folding chair. I held it above the can and used the toothbrush to brush off the powdery mess into the can.

Mrs. Leviticus stood and watched until I'd finished the third row. Boredom overcame her gloating her and she left, taking the canister vacuum with her. The room had one camera that I spotted. It was of the pinhole variety and hidden over the screen at the front of the room.

Fortunately for me, the prime wife was indiscriminate about where she sprayed her instant mess. It looked as if the flour and breadcrumbs stuck to the hole, which meant the camera was blocked. They couldn't see what I was doing until I cleaned it and I wasn't about to do that.

Time to MacGyver up something to speed up the cleaning.

Maybe I could sup up the fans on the overhead projector to blow the mess into one corner of the room and use some folders as a dustpan to scoop the mess into the garbage. Shouldn't take more than a few hours. If I could figure a way to separate the sugar, I could make it into a syrup to coat the walls and the ceiling so they'd shine.

I was halfway to the projector when the door behind the podium opened a crack. Whispered arguing leaked through. It seemed that several folks on the other side of the door all wanted to be the first to peek.

The whispers all sounded male so I wasn't surprised when I flung open the door and four Deep Ones fell to the floor, each one landing on top of another.

They looked young with none of the extra folds of skin and scales that happened as Deep Ones aged. I put them at having turned recently turned which probably put them between twenty-five to thirty-five years old.

Judging by the whispers I'd overheard, they were all eligible to choose a bride and wanted to check me out.

With all respect to Tom Sawyer, I now had a way to get the work done while I searched the building for the page of the Necronomicon.

It's wrong and stereotypical. but a lot of men in many species are easily convinced that blondes can be vapid. While there may be a few who do fit the stereotype, many more of us have learned how to use that stereotype to our advantage. I dialed up my smile and dialed down my perceived intelligence.

"What are you guys doing here? I didn't expect to see so many strapping and handsome men in one place," I cooed. The embarrassment over the fall transformed into awkward hope that perhaps I might be interested in one of them. "What are you all doing here?"

The young Deep Ones awkwardly brushed themselves off. As they rose to their feet, the shortest of the bunch stepped forward to try out the first story he'd come up with. "We thought there was a prayer meeting but I guess we must've gotten our times or days mixed up."

I giggled. "That happens to me all the time. I was wondering when I was going to get to meet all the eligible bachelors but didn't think I'd get this lucky so soon."

The Deep Ones all stood up a little straighter, puffing out their chests and sucking in their guts. A gut on a Deep One wasn't necessarily a sign of being out of shape. It was the way their bodies were shaped. It looked like one of them didn't get that memo and was wearing abdominal shapewear.

The tallest spoke up. "Well, this isn't an official mixer, but we heard about you joining and wanted to make sure we got to welcome you in person."

I gave a quick bounce on my heels, followed by placing my hands over my chest, which is where the four of them were looking anyway. "That's just so sweet of you all. I'd love the chance to chat and get to know you. Maybe even find out the rules about having one or more you take me on a date, so we can get to know each other better but I'm afraid right now I just can't."

The one in the elastic girdle substitute frowned. "But why? We've got the whole day free."

"The whole night too," said the fourth Deep One who had darker scales above his lip that looked like a mustache.

I sighed and slumped my shoulders. I motioned to the powder-covered room. "Unfortunately, I have to clean all this before I could do anything else. I was told I couldn't leave until everything shined enough so that Mrs. Leviticus could see her face in it."

"What a frightening thought," Shorty said. The others chuckled.

"Who knows how much longer it will take me to get through? It's too bad that I won't be at the get to know any of you better until that official mixer."

"But that won't be until you're six months into your time," Girdle said.

I shrugged and put my hands up to my side. "It stinks but I have to follow the rules and do what I'm told in order to join the church. Although I'd love to hang out with all of you."

"We'd love to hang out with you," said Stretch.

I know I'd be criticized by a lot of feminists for what I was about to do but there was a world to save.

I crossed my arms in front of me and held my left wrist with my right hand and started rocking my torso left to right. "If there was only some way that this job could get done faster so all of us could hang out together."

"We could clean it for you," Mustache said.

I put my best surprised-yet-happy expression on my face and gently touched Mustache's elbow. "You'd do that for me?"

"Of course. You never know. If things go right, maybe you and I end up married a year from now. What kind of future husband would I be if I didn't help the woman who might someday be my wife?"

I nodded slowly. "That's so smart. I certainly would be indebted to anyone who would do so much for me."

The other three exchanged looks and practically jumped forward.

"We'll help too!" Shorty said.

"Darn right we will," Stretch said.

"Absolutely," agreed Girdle.

"Your kindness and generosity are enough to make a girl blush. Do you think you could find stuff to clean this place up like vacuums, mops, and buckets?" And now that I had help, there was a better option than covering the place in a sugar glaze. "Do you think you could also get some brushes, rolling pins, and a few gallons of a clear glossy varnish?"

"I can do better than that. I have a paint sprayer from my time working as a contractor. We can use that to make the walls and ceiling shine with the varnish," Shorty said.

"You wait here, Bikini, and we'll be right back and take care of all this for you," Girdle said as the four of them rushed off.

28

They were back shortly and got to work.

Less than twenty minutes later, I was roaming the halls of the compound. The Deep Boys had gotten everything they promised and were going to town on getting rid of the powder before they started on the varnishing. I suggested we clean the area by the hidden camera last so they would didn't get caught helping me. They were agreeable.

I excused myself to go to the bathroom and headed toward the area I felt the urge to avoid.

I walked the halls like I owned the place. The worst thing you can do is be caught sneaking around because people will find that suspicious. But act like you belonged, a lot of the time people won't bother you.

I didn't have much worry about the security cameras. My earrings not only had cameras and recording devices but also jammers. Once they were turned on, they'd freeze the video image on any digital device for a few seconds until I passed by. While it didn't work well in crowded areas where people were moving, for empty hallways it was fantastic.

The doors and elevators worked off the chips in the ID cards people wore.

They hadn't given me one of my own which I'm sure they thought would limit me to whatever area they left me in. Might have even worked if I hadn't pickpocketed the badge from the limo driver when I bumped into him, then swapped it out with the one Mrs. Leviticus had. I figured she had clearance to almost the whole compound.

With any luck, the chauffeur wouldn't come back inside the building until his shift was done or notice his badge was missing until then.

I contemplated going to each floor—I'd counted how many on my way in. But every fiber of my being screamed to avoid the penthouse.

I could take the elevator but the jammers in my earrings would show nobody in the moving elevator. If I didn't use them, security would see that I wasn't Mrs. Leviticus. I didn't see the prime wife as someone who was trying to get extra steps in so if I used her badge to open the stairwell door, it might seem odd.

There was another option that didn't involve climbing up the outside of the building.

I was amazed by people who spent a fortune on digital electronic security features and still use basic doors. I slid the ID card into the doorjamb and popped open the locking mechanism.

I slid a magnetic sticker onto the door sensor so the alarm wouldn't sound. I had stuck several of them on my hip earlier in the day. Since they were attached to me instead of the bikini, they wouldn't disappear if my bikini changed.

I used another sticker to make sure the latch didn't go back into the strike plate so I could get out quickly.

From down the hall, I heard Leviticus's voice. He hadn't bothered to close the door.

"I am truly sorry, Chief Flag, but you knew the risks and you took the money. As long as you keep quiet about my involvement, I'll be happy to contribute lawyers to your cause and more than likely be able to prevent any charges from being filed, although it may result in your losing your job."

"What about my pension? And my reputation?" Flag's voice sounded like he was on a phone speaker.

"Neither are under my control. The money I gave you should be enough to make sure you will live comfortably for the rest of your life." Of course, Flag probably didn't realize that when someone like the Reverend Leviticus said that, he was likely implying that the police chief would be killed soon. Otherwise, he would have said for years to come or some such.

Megalomaniacs love to show smart they are by telling people what they are going to do to them.

I felt the urge to run. The page was in there.

"Listen here, Leviticus…" Flag shouted.

"I've listened enough. I have someplace I need to be." Without so much as a goodbye, the reverend ended the phone call with the crooked cop.

Steps followed, so I dashed around the corner away from the elevator and climbed up a wall with my hands on one side and my feet on the other until I was suspended near the ceiling.

With luck, Leviticus was headed in the other direction to take the elevator. If he wasn't, he might not look up. If he did, hopefully I'd get the drop on him. Literally.

His steps went away from me and the elevator opened and closed again. I went back to the office but the urge to flee was gone. That meant only one thing. Leviticus was carrying the page somewhere on his person.

As the page would grant him the power to defend it, a direct assault was a bad idea. I dropped onto the floor and went inside the office. There was no computer in the room but that was a smart move because there were so many ways a computer could be hacked these days from the mundane to the magical. It just wasn't a good place to store sensitive information unless you had ridiculously secure firewalls and wards.

Leviticus had an old-fashioned calendar blotter on top of the desk. There was only one thing marked for the entire month. It was tomorrow at 10 AM and was accented by a smiley face.

Now I knew the when. The where was some place that water touched Manhattan. All that was left was to stop him from summoning Dagon Junior.

I retraced my steps quickly back to the conference room. The place was clean from the powdery mess, but only three walls were shiny and the Deep Boys were nowhere to be seen. Once I stepped into the room, Mrs. Leviticus stepped out of the closet glaring.

"I knew you couldn't be trusted."

Before I could try to give an excuse, twin needles pierced my bare abdomen followed by the jolt of a high-output Taser.

Convulsions and blackness enveloped me before I hit the floor.

29

I regained consciousness in large part thanks to a horrible headache and searing pain above my navel.

I've been in this situation before. Often there's somebody watching. It's never a good idea to let them know I'm awake right off the bat so I didn't open my eyes all the way or look around. Instead, I did my best to relax my muscles and not to vary my breathing, while opening my eyelids just a smidge.

Wherever I was, it was dark, so I slowly open my eyes the rest of the way. The floor under me felt like tile. Very carefully, I reached out around me with my arms and legs and felt nothing besides more floor.

Rolling onto my back, I lifted my legs in the air and didn't bump into anything. You'd be surprised how many people sit up in the dark and get smashed back into unconsciousness by smacking their heads into something.

There were no clues as to what time it was. Or what day for that matter. I slowly stood up with my arms reached above my head. By the time I got to my tiptoes, my fingers were still touching only air. I strained my eyes for all the good it did me. Wherever I was, there wasn't even a flicker of light, but I could fix that.

I stripped out of my bikini top and bottom and focused hard so that the next bikini that appeared on my body had a few special properties, the most important of which was its fluorescence.

I was more than familiar enough with several materials that would give off light, so I picked the least dangerous of them. Translation—one that wasn't radioactive. I went with *panellis stipticus*, better known as bitter oyster. It's the brightest of the bioluminescent fungi. It may not have been radioactive, but it was still a fungus so I made sure there was a layer of padding between the green glowing fungus and my skin.

I noted with amusement that the bikini I took off wasn't pink but red. Mrs. Leviticus must have tried to dress me while I was unconscious. The woman had issues—besides the obvious one of being part of a doomsday cult that treated women as second-class citizens. Although she was the head of those second-class citizens, so maybe she was of the mind that it was better to rule in hell than serve in heaven. She was probably doing a little of both.

Now that I could see, I wasn't very impressed.

It was a small room. Probably cell would be a better description. It was about eight by eight feet with the ceiling clocking in at maybe ten feet. It was slightly smaller than my cell at Rikers, although none of the space was taken up by any niceties like a bunk or toilet. Not even a bucket, which was a bad thing. However long I'd been out, it was enough time that my bladder felt full.

That's something you never read about in books or see in movies. When a hero wakes up after being unconscious for a long time, they never have to answer nature's call. Or maybe they took care of it while they were unconscious. As anybody knows, it's really hard to focus on anything else when you need to use the bathroom. Sure, I could go in the corner or make a bikini diaper, but I didn't know how long I was going to be trapped and nothing ruins captivity more than the stink of your own bodily waste.

The walls which were lined with what felt like a thin sheet of metal laid over what was likely sheetrock, but it was thick enough that I couldn't punch or kick through it. The door had a rubber liner to block out any outside light. My side of the door had no sign of a lock or doorknob. It was undoubtedly very sturdy, probably designed so that if someone felt it in the dark, it would give the impression of permanence to the imprisonment.

I stomped my feet as quietly as I could on the floor. It felt solid.

That left the ceiling.

There was a small gap in one corner where the metal wasn't completely flush and had a small gap. It wasn't much, but it was some place to start. I slipped off my glowing bikini and focused hard on the one that came next.

When it appeared, I carefully eased off the bottom and then unfastened the top from the back and slid it down my arms making sure no part of my skin touched the front of the cups. The reason I was so careful was that the fronts of the cups were covered in Vegargantuan spider webbing. It was the most adhesive substance I'd ever even heard of and lasts for upwards of a century. It is notoriously hard to dissolve unless you can also get a hold of the saliva from the parent Vegargantuan spider.

Next, I twisted and separated the cups and carefully placed one at waist level and the other at head level so the cups covered all the webbing. An identical bikini appeared. I repeated the removal process as I focused on what type of bikini would come next.

Stepping in the strap on the lowest cup, I then stepped into the strap of the one above it as I placed the bikini cup in my left hand up high on the wall making. Hanging onto that I pulled myself up with my left hand so I could place the last cup on the metal corner of the ceiling. Once it was stuck there firmly, I grabbed hold of the ceiling cup strap and jumped towards the floor. The straps were reinforced and my weight pulled the metal corner free.

Holding tight to the strap, I swung back and forth like a trapeze artist, turning to push off the corner with my feet and holding on tight. I repeated until there was enough ceiling exposed for me to fit through. That is if it wasn't for the sheetrock underneath.

My new bikini had a metal belt designed to resemble the teeth on a saw. I took it off and it sprang itself straight.

Climbing back up my bikini cup ladder, I held onto the top one with my left hand and used my right to saw through the sheetrock, hoping they hadn't encased the outside with metal as well. Once I cut through enough, I reached my fingers in and pulled a chunk free.

It was a normal ceiling!

There was just enough room to drop something between the outer sheetrock and the hall.

I climbed to the floor and took off yet another bikini. The new one was covered in a form of nitroglycerin. Yes, I could've focused on a stronger explosive to try to blow out the door but the explosion might knock down the reinforced entrance and if it didn't, the shockwave would blow back and bounce off the metal walls, going through me each time and turning my insides to jelly.

Beings able to summon specialized bikinis out of thin air is really the only part of the curse that ever helps me out, but it has its limits. I can't get a bikini that works like a gun or cell phone. Forming most machinery is beyond the curse's scope.

The nitroglycerin variant exploded on impact. I made sure not to add any shrapnel. There were no metal clasps, only Velcro. I needed to blow a hole in the wall, not kill any guards in the hall.

I took off the explosive bikini and did a layup, then dove for cover.

The blast was loud, even through my hands which were covering my ears. I leapt up, climbed the ladder of sticky bikini cups, and peaked down. A huge section of sheetrock was gone. I shimmed through the opening in the ceiling and dropped down on the other side.

I looked out into the hall. Two Deep One were covering their ears and stumbling.

I didn't have time for anything fancy so I took them both out with a pair of *I got your nose* nerve pinches, a signature move of the Shadow Clowns.

Each had a Glock in a shoulder holster. Too easy to kill with a gun so rather than keep them, I removed the clips and tossed them up through the ceiling hole into my cell, then disassembled the guns into their component pieces then sent them off into the cell.

I grabbed both their ID cards and a cell phone off one. Security was set as fingerprint scan so I lifted his limp hand and opened the phone.

I couldn't get an outside signal. Leviticus was probably running a jammer. It was connected to the Internet via wi-fi but it was severely restricted. Basically, it allowed only the church's own app which only let them text each other.

Communicating that I was free to my captors wasn't on my agenda. I need out of the building fast. No audible alarm despite the explosion. What was the best way out? I was woozy, so after a very quick visit to the rest room—you try to fight when you have to pee—I decided on the elevator.

The first ID badge opened the elevator doors. If I could believe the number over the door, I was on the sixth floor.

The elevator was a risk—they could stop it and trap me, especially if they saw me on the camera. This was a religious cult compound that probably didn't see a lot of high espionage acts. With any luck, I'd be out of the building before they figured out what was happening.

Or there could be a swarm of armed Deep Ones waiting in the lobby when the elevator doors opened.

Guess which one happened?

30

Being forced to always wear a bikini has a lot of downsides, but sometimes in a fight, it's an advantage. Untrained fighters who like women are often so busy looking at my body that it slows their reaction time.

And these Deep Ones seemed to fall in that category.

As I stepped out of the elevator, I was reminded that smoking is a dirty habit. Apparently, Deep Ones weren't scared of little things like lung cancer because there was a garbage can with an ashtray on top that was full of the smoked remains of dozens of cigarettes. I grabbed the tray and flicked ash into the face of the Deep One nearest me, then threw it like a frisbee into the nose of the next scaly gunman.

Taking advantage of them not being able to see for the moment, I did twin neural jabs to their dominant brachial plexuses followed by one to their solar plexuses. They doubled over in pain, gasping for breath with numb arms which let me pluck the guns out of their hands with no resistance.

Using the one with ash in his eyes as a shield, I shot at the hands of the next two nearest Deep Ones.

I'd like to say I shot the guns out of their hands, but that kind of skill is rare. Not only that, but if the gun isn't hit at the right angle, the gun doesn't drop and someone can be hit by a ricochet.

However, a flesh wound to the hand will make someone drop a gun almost every time.

My inhuman shield turned to attack me, so I stuck two fingers into what passed for his nostrils and pulled down hard as I rammed my other palm my palm into his jaw. He hit the ground.

I ran between the two Deep Ones holding their bloody hands, hoping the other gunmen wouldn't risk hitting their companions.

There were six more armed Deep Ones in the lobby, but only two of them were between me and the door. I made like I was going to jump over them, so they aimed their guns high. Instead, I slid across the waxed floor on my butt and boots—bare skin and sliding don't mix well—and slammed the gun barrels into their groins.

A word to the critics and haters who'd complain that this was fighting dirty. They were trying to kill me and I was trying to stop the slaughter of millions. Even a kindergartener could do that math. And there is no such thing as fighting dirty when you are trying to survive. Plus, I could have taken the easier and quicker route and popped a bullet into each of their skulls.

I didn't.

The pair bent over and grabbed their crotches. I smashed each gun barrel into the side of a head, knocking them out.

A woman behind the security desk yelled, "The doors are sealed shut. You are not getting out, Harlot of America!"

I smiled and emptied both guns at a window panel to the side of the door, shattering it. I looked back and dropped the guns. "That's okay. I was born by Caesarian section so I prefer leaving by a window anyway."

I jumped through and the cell phone I'd taken from the guard fell out of my bikini top. I know it's not classy, but where else was I going to put it? They started shooting so there was no going back for it. And they'd taken my earrings when I was unconscious, so nobody at Bikini Tower knew what was happening.

I sprinted away down Battery Place.

31

I turned a corner and reached up to take out the tie that was holding my ponytail in place. In my hand, it reverted into a writhing worm.

I whispered, "Which way should I go to stop the summoning?"

The worm swayed reminding me of a cobra summoned out of a basket by the song of a snake charmer. It shimmered and shock until the vibrations sounded like words. "Bikini Jones, is this the favor you ask of me?"

"Queen of Worms, it is not."

"Then I cannot tell you as doing so would appear to Dagon's spawn as if I am taking sides against it."

"That's one way to look at it. Another would be that I'm the only shot Earth has of stopping this extra-dimensional incursion. Dagon Junior's arrival is imminent. Even though you don't believe I have much of a chance of preventing it, you haven't said I had none. If I beat the odds like I have so many times before and stop it, not only is the human populace spared but so are you."

The worm trembled and vibrated again. "We elder things are bound by laws that must be followed exactly so we tend to think in absolutes. I do not see a way around my answer leading the spawn to think I have moved against it."

"What if instead of telling me where the ritual is going to be performed, you instead point out to me exactly where I should avoid going so I don't interfere?"

The vibrating giggle the worm made sent shivers down my spine. The Queen of Worms used no words but the top of the worm pointed south so I started running in that direction. At each corner, I watched carefully to see if I needed to turn or keep going straight.

An old stone building had a clock set in a wall.

9:48.

Twelve minutes left to prevent the end of New York City and maybe the world.

I ran faster. The worm was pointing directly toward Battery Park where they had the ferry to go to the Statue of Liberty and

Ellis Island.

I figured out where we were head heading—Castle Clinton.

Not a traditional castle, it's a circular sandstone structure that was only a small parking lot's distance from the water. It was a fort built in the early 1800s that transitioned to welcoming immigrants before the task was moved to Ellis Island. It also housed the New York City aquarium before it moved to Coney Island in 1941.

As places to perform a summoning in NYC go, it was a smart choice as it was fairly easy to keep people out, especially as the entrance was being blocked by a half dozen Deep Ones dressed in long black robes and carrying AR-15s. Not a cop in sight. Maybe Chief Flag had something to do with that.

I was guessing we were down to five minutes and it would take me at least that long to deal with the armed cultists so I went around the side and parkoured my way up the sandstone wall and onto the top of the outer wall.

The worm wrapped itself around my finger as if it were a ring. I guessed that meant I'd arrived.

At the center of the garden inside the fort, there was a mystic circle with Deep One cultists in black robes holding hands and chanting. In the center stood the Reverend Leviticus. The only one not robed, he wore another ridiculously expensive suit. The page from the Necronomicon was in his hand and he was chanting in ancient Sumerian. I only knew the basics but didn't like what I heard.

Below him was the unconscious form of Isaac. The SOB was going to sacrifice his son to open a breach into the dimension of darkness.

I dropped from the wall to the ground and started running, using my best Shadow Clown techniques to avoid being seen, but there are limits to how invisible one can be in broad daylight running across a large open space.

The best I could manage was total silence and limiting any motion that would draw eyes. I'm not claiming that I didn't pick Mrs. Leviticus as the weakest link to get into the circle but I'd be lying if I said I'd didn't get a great deal of pleasure from hitting her in her occiput with an open palm then running over her limp body.

If the Reverend Leviticus knew I was there, he didn't show it. Instead, he pulled a long sacrificial knife from beneath his suit and sliced downward across Isaac's chest repeatedly, carving a symbol similar to the one that summoned Dagon with a couple of minor differences. The sky above us darkened and a bolt of darkness shot from the Necronomicon page towards my chest. If I'd been a millisecond slower, it would have killed me. I kicked Leviticus from behind and he slammed face-first into the grass but the page flew up from his hand and shot more mystical bolts at me.

I wasn't a witch, wizard, or sorcerer but I had more than a little familiarity with magic. With the right spell, a lot of dedication, and practice, not to mention a strong will, anybody can learn to do magic. I'd been drawing ancient runes since Odin taught me after I'd freed him from the third rail that Baba Yaga had tied him to. It had started as yet another masochistic attempt by the one-eyed Norse god to get even more knowledge but the Russian witch then tried to steal the knowledge and Odin's life. The knowledge he taught me as a reward has come in handy more than once. Sadly, these runes only work in the presence of magic, which limited their use.

I drew a symbol in the air in front of me and a glowing shield appeared to absorb the bolts

A portal opened in the sky and a shadowy, nebulous mass reached down toward the unconscious and bleeding Isaac, forming into tentacles.

The shield could shoot back what it absorbed, so I fired the dark magic back and vaporized the longest three inky tentacles, but dozens more followed.

The page realized what had happened and didn't fire any more bolts for me to use as ammunition. I watched helplessly as one tendril reached down and made contact with the blood spilling from the symbol sliced in the teen's scaly chest.

The shadows surged and were then sucked through the cuts into Isaac's body until the darkness was gone from sight.

There was no stopping the incursion now. The thing of darkness had a living host to anchor him to our plane. Dagon Junior was coming.

Isaac floated up from the ground toward the portal. I leapt to grab hold of the teenager's feet but the hands of dozens of cultists grabbed onto my legs. I wasn't strong enough to support their weight added to mine so my grip slipped and I fell, spinning on the way down. I lashed out with my arms and legs. By the time I hit the ground, so did seven cultists of The Church of the Majestic Deep. There had been fifteen making up the circle at the start. Counting limp Mrs. Leviticus, that left seven conscious cultists.

There was a Shadow Clown move that would have let me take them all out in seconds but I didn't have my big clown shoes or a seltzer bottle with me.

Under ideal circumstances, I try to talk and reason with an opponent but anybody willing to take part in a ceremony that at the very least would kill everybody in the tri-state area inside of hours or days was beyond pity or reason. Or mercy for that matter. I didn't hold back. It was all over in about two minutes. The cultists would live but none would enjoy a day without pain ever again.

Assuming any of us were still alive tomorrow

By this point, Isaac's body was floating over the water in front of the dock the ferries launched from. The portal followed and dropped down to meet him.

I frisked a cultist, then reached under his black robe and pulled out a cell phone. Another moron who used his fingerprint as a passcode. A second later I was in and I dialed my emergency line. Nobody but me had the number.

Stanley picked up on the first ring. "Bikini, are you okay?"

"I'm fine but New York isn't going to be for long. I need *The Brass Ring* in the air with any volunteers from the tower willing to help fight the incursion of a spawn of an elder thing at Battery Park."

"How big is it?"

I looked at Isaac. "Man-sized at the moment but I suspect the height will be measured in stories in minutes."

"I'll sound the alarm."

As I moved toward Leviticus, the half-dozen scaly storm troopers who had been guarding were rushing with their guns pointing at me.

I did the only logical thing and moved so Reverend Leviticus—who was struggling to his feet—was between me and gun-toting cultists.

"Tremble, Bikini Jones! The spawn of Dagon is loosed upon the Earth and soon I will be a god!" It was the typical rant of someone looking to do anything to grab the tiniest bit of power.

"So you're willing to sell out humanity to lick Dagon Junior's scaly toes?" I said, moving so Leviticus followed me, unable to see his soldiers approaching.

"What have humans done for my kind besides looked down and persecute us?"

"Besides a bunch of them joining your cult and some bearing your children?" The half dozen gun welding Deep Ones were now close enough to hear our conversation. "What about your kind? Your people are considered children of Dagon, but this is his first-begotten spawn. There is undoubtedly going to be some sibling rivalry. I suspect Junior will kill off Deep Ones every bit as easily as he will humans, whether they're in your cult or not."

In the classic gesture of not caring, Leviticus threw his arms up to the side and his shoulders toward his ears. "What does anyone else matter as long as I get what is coming to me? Surely you don't think I care more about my worshipers than my flesh and blood son? If I was willing to offer up Isaac as a sacrifice to bring the spawn of Dagon and grant his darkness form, why would I care about some dunderheads dumb enough to give me everything? If I tell them they need to die to serve our master, then, by Dagon, they will line up and plead to be the first to the slaughter."

"So to be perfectly clear, you have no plan of protecting anyone else besides yourself? Not your wife, daughter, or any members of The Church of the Majestic Deep?"

Leviticus laughed as if that was the funniest thing he'd ever heard. "In this world and the one about to be forged in Dagon's image, I will have to look out for myself. Let everyone else do the same."

The cultists behind Leviticus stopped pointing their guns at me and exchanged glances. Their expressions were not happy.

"So you won't share the power of your new position to offer protection for those in your church?"

Leviticus shrugged. "I might to those who are strong enough to survive. After all, I'm going to need servants and slaves in the new world I will rule. Vow to serve me now, Bikini Jones, I will allow you to survive as one of my concubines."

The sky was flashing from dark lightning pouring out of the portal.

"Thank you for such a disgusting and creepy offer. Hard pass."

I made a show of looking over his shoulder. "What about you boys? Would you like to survive the coming Apocalypse by being concubines for your leader?"

The amphibiman in the expensive suit suddenly wasn't laughing anymore as he turned and saw six of his trusted soldiers pointing their AR-15s at him.

"How much of that did you hear?" Leviticus asked.

"Enough for us to know to make sure that you don't live to see the Apocalypse either," the largest of the cultists said.

Leviticus raised his hands above his shoulders. "I was just trying to talk Bikini Jones into surrendering."

"It didn't sound that way to me," the biggest Deep One grumbled. "How about the rest of you?"

They all agreed that they didn't believe their leader.

"So now that you guys know the real score, I've got to go stop Dagon Junior from fully forming and killing us all. Maybe even see if we can't send it back and save the world." And maybe even Isaac, but it may be too late for that.

"That sounds like a real good idea. We were promised a place of power in the coming world, not death. Do what you have to do. We won't interfere," the big Deep One said.

Leviticus was so stunned by this turn of events—especially since he would not be granted power until Dagon Junior was fully formed—that I was able to pluck the sacrificial dagger and the page of the Necronomicon out of his hands before he could react. The page let me as its entire purpose in summoning Dagon Junior had been completed, so its purpose and power were spent.

I left Leviticus to the tender mercy mercies of his fellow church members.

Truth be told, I had less sympathy for them than the reverend. They were all willing to sell out the Earth for a place in the world after the Apocalypse, but Leviticus would at least have gotten godhood. Those morons would just get to be residents.

32

I parkoured my way up the wall nearest the water and froze. New York Harbor was bubbling like someone boiling water mixed with explosives.

Speaking of explosives, I could use some now. A heck of a lot more than I could get from an exploding bikini. Dagon was a sea-based entity, so it seemed a safe bet that his spawn would be too. Given that Junior had Isaac's body as an anchor in this world and Deep Ones had links to the water, I was going with that as fact.

My guess for the tumultuous water was Junior had submerged Isaac's body and was transforming anything organic in the saltwater into an absorbable mass to let him enlarge his form. The only way to stop it would be to get Isaac's body out of the water and far away.

I had no way to do that. Instead, I parkoured down the wall and ran across the parking lot. The Hudson River was churning red. Any marine life nearby was being killed and absorbed.

Thank goodness we had evacuated the shark people.

The sky was lit by a ball of glowing light heading towards me. It was a foo fighter, specifically my foo fighter ship developed by a race of fey that mixed tech and magic expertly. It traveled at insane speeds and could make right-angle turns. It landed next to me and a door opened to reveal Stanley inside.

"Hey, boss. Aditte is gathering up the troops in the tower but I figured you might need a few things in the meantime." Stanley motioned with his arm towards the small interior of the foo fighter. "Take your pick."

As Stanley stepped out of the ship I went in and smiled at what I saw. I put on a replacement watch first. "I knew there was a reason I kept you around."

"And here I thought it was because I made the best caramel mocha lattes in Manhattan."

"That too," I admitted as I slipped on a jetpack. It didn't use jets but did negate gravity and allow the wearer to fly. The harness was similar in design to that of a parachute but made with transparent straps. I put it on and the pack was ten inches away from my back, resting on a transparent block. In short, my bikini could still be seen, so the curse didn't kick in and make the jetpack disappear, which would be a bad thing to happen several hundred feet in the air.

The straps also held transparent holsters in which I placed a pair of energy blaster pistols. I slid the sacrificial dagger along with the page from the Necronomicon and sealed it in a transparent pouch in the harness. I put on a pair of wrist rocket launcher gauntlets. Each held six lipstick-sized rockets powerful enough to blow a hole in a cement bunker. Lastly, I picked up a weapon the size of a bazooka that could disintegrate a city bus. It was science-based and things from the dark dimension utilized energy more akin to magic which often not only broke but completely ignored the laws of physics so there was no way of telling how effective it would be.

"What you need me to do now, boss?" Stanley was amazing at keeping my day-to-day life organized. Plus, he was brave and had a good heart, but he didn't have any powers to speak of or any special fighting skills beyond the mandated training all employees of Bikini Enterprises and Bikini Foundation had to take. Asking him to join in this fight would be akin to suggesting he become a kamikaze, which would still have no effect on Dagon Junior.

"Use the foo fighter speakers and tell those people to get out of here. Then get on the horn with the Mayor and tell him to evacuate any parts of the city near the water. Then tell the governor of New Jersey to do the same."

"Just the shorelines?"

"That'll stop people being killed in a crossfire but if we don't stop it here and now, nobody's going to get far enough away to do much good." Dagon Junior was starting out relatively small, but as he killed people, he would absorb their life force and bodies. Junior would grow until he could look down on the Empire State Building.

"Oh joy. Then I guess you better stop yapping and buckle down and save the world again."

"That's the plan," I said.

Stanley tried not to show any fear, but I watched as his pupils grew and absorbed his irises. "That's not the entire plan, right?"

"At the moment, it kind of is. But I'm good at improvising." I slipped a band around my head which formed a mental link between me and the jetpack which allowed me to fly it without any other external controls.

I lifted into the sky. "Stanley, quit lollygagging and get moving."

"On it, boss." Speaking into his Bluetooth ear pods, he was telling his phone to call the mayor as he got back in the foo fighter.

I hovered over the bubbling water as the foo fighter flew around the people on the docks. Stanley's voice boomed telling them to stop being stupid and run the hell away. Most of them listened. Others were too busy filming on their phones hoping for their moment of social media fame.

I couldn't see anything through the churning Hudson so I aimed the energy bazooka at the center of the disturbance, figuring that's where Dagon Junior would be.

I did it knowing full well that if it worked, it would likely kill Isaac too. Even though it tore me up inside, I still pulled the trigger. One life versus millions, maybe billions. Sometimes the math of protecting life will break your heart.

The water glowed and turned to steam. The churning slowed.

Even though everything I knew told me there was no way stopping Junior would be that easy, I allowed myself to hope.

The water erupted and I barely flew out of the way in time. A huge scaly monster rose from the Hudson River.

The energy blast may have interrupted Dagon Junior's growth spurt, but I wished I'd been able to shoot sooner. My best guess was that Junior had topped out at ten stories, with green scaly skin, a giant fin on the top of his head, jaws that could snap a subway car, and clawed webbed hands that could swat me like I was a fly. Judging by his roar, he was not happy I'd interrupted his growth spurt.

Being ticked off would be bad news for whatever he focused his anger on. I had to make sure it was me and not New York City so I fired my energy cannon again, aiming for his left eye. I was close, maybe about three feet off but that's the advantage of an energy weapon–I could just correct my aim.

A moment later the energy beam cooked his eyeball, which was easily as big as the foo fighter.

That made me the object of his fury. A huge clawed and webbed hand swiped towards the section of the sky I had been in an instant before. That's the beauty of a neural interface—there's no lag time like there is when you have to physically move controls.

The energy cannon needed a few minutes to build up enough of a charge. I hung it over my neck with its strap—also transparent for obvious reasons—so it hung by my side. And I pulled out a blaster with my right hand and pointed my left wrist gauntlet towards the creature. I fired off four lipstick-sized wrist rockets at his open mouth and tried for his other eye with a blaster. The rockets hit, giving him a bloody lip and the equivalent of a cavity or two but he was faster now. Junior turned his head so my blaster beam hit him between the eyes, and it just made him bleed a thick black ooze that barely seemed to irate the monster.

I shot up to put some sky between us, but Junior's eyes looked behind me and he stopped moving.

I followed his gaze. Dagon Junior was staring at the Statue of Liberty. It took me a moment to figure out why.

Dagon Junior took on the attributes of his host's physical form, not unlike the Queen of Worms. In this case, instead of an invertebrate Junior got a horny teenager and Lady Liberty was the only woman anywhere near his size. The growth spurt had destroyed Isaac's clothing and Dagon Junior was standing in the Hudson River in all his natural glory. Not that I wanted to look, but it was obvious that he liked the large green woman on Bedloe's Island.

Diving down, I concentrated my rockets on one of his knees while he was distracted. I would've preferred the Achilles tendon, but it was still underwater.

My attack had barely made Junior stumble, I refocused my fire on more tender parts of the male anatomy. You already know my thoughts on fighting dirty when lives were on the line. Junior would soon head toward dry land to devour and absorb the citizens of New York, so I needed to do anything I could to stop him.

This attack caused a roar as the leviathan hunched over and grabbed for his groin. Unfortunately, he then grabbed one of the ferries, which thanks to Stanley's constant yelling was free of passengers and crew. Junior made like a quarterback and I was his wide receiver. The ferry flew at me. I moved into reverse as fast as the jetpack could carry me. I almost got clear, but the guard rail clipped my right hand, knocking my gun away. Both the ferry and my blaster hit the Hudson hard.

My fingers were numb from the impact. I needed a way to hold Dagon Junior or get him away from the city. He'd never stay still long enough to get him in a containment cube but maybe I could lure him out of the harbor and into the open ocean. Sure, on the one webbed hand that gave access to tons of fish he could absorb to grow even larger but it would stop him from killing and absorbing people. At least in the short term.

Before I could dream up anything brilliant, I heard the sounds of the William Tell Overture blasting through the city and I smiled. Aditte loved to play the theme song from a certain legendary masked cowboy when she was coming to rescue me. *The Brass Ring* dropped out of the sky and blasted Dagon Junior in the chest. As the building-sized man-fish hadn't been prepared, the blow knocked him on his scaly butt.

Junior didn't lay down for long. Within seconds, he was struggling to regain his footing which is when *The Brass Ring* opened its bay doors. Tapedo and over two dozen shark people dropped from the sky onto the gigantic sea monster and began using their jaws to rip pieces of flesh from whatever part of his body they landed on. They were followed by Shrill's mechanical form using hand and foot blasters to lower herself down, with her much larger husband Crunch on her back. He was still in a suit but now was holding a broadsword taller and wider than I was. The ogre jumped off his wife's back to land at the base of Dagon Junior's head. The ogre plunged the huge broadsword into the space between his axis and his occiput. In layperson's terms, he stabbed between the highest vertebrae of the spine and his skull.

Junior's left arm went limp.

Shrill flew near his left ear which she blasted with ultrasonics. Deep Ones still had most of the same basic anatomy as humans, including the semicircular canals in the ear. The ultrasonics hit them hard and made Dagon Junior wobble like he was drunk.

A minivan flew through the air to hit Dagon Junior in his stomach. I looked towards the shore and saw my doorman Sherman picking up another car to launch. He may have been short and over eighty, but his cybernetics made him insanely mighty. That's when I noticed my biggest surprise–a thirty-foot tall robotic ape walking through Battery Park, then jumping into the Hudson River.

It was barely a third of Dagon Junior's size but that didn't stop it from launching a barrage of punches on his right leg, focusing on the knee. One of the flurries of blows dislocated Junior's kneecap and that leg buckled, but the colossus didn't fall.

The enormous ape robot head gave me a nod.

I recognized the mech. Chimpazoid's head briefly housed Dr. Dendrite's brain a few years back. I thought the US military had destroyed it after he used it to attack Albuquerque, but it seems I was wrong. Even from a distance, I could see that one of his ears had been made into a hatch, which meant that doggy Dendrites hadn't transplanted his brain but was piloting the thing from inside its metallic skull.

There were some screams from the shoreline. A familiar one-eyed green and tentacled creature was heading toward some tourists and locals who hadn't evacuated as they were too busy recording the happenings for prosperity on their phones and social media. Jenny was using her telekinetic abilities to lift them up and away from the immediate danger zone.

An energy cannon blast hit Junior in the Adam's apple. Hany was airborne with another jetpack, blasting the leviathan with a second energy cannon.

We had stopped Junior from attacking Manhattan but only thanks to the element of surprise and teamwork. Junior would be able to overcome that soon and we'd lose our advantage.

I held my worm ring up in front of my face.

"Queen of Worms, we need your help," I shouted.

"Is this your favor, Bikini Jones?" the worm hummed.

"Yes, it is."

The worm vibrated some more. "You have no objections to me escaping from this pitiful mortal prison?"

"I don't." I'd do everything in my power to smooth it over with the Department of Corrections later. Assuming we survived.

Rikers Island was west of the opposite end of Manhattan, offshore between Queens and the Bronx. I expected ten or fifteen minutes to pass, as even the Queen of Worms would have to deal with New York City traffic.

Boy, was I wrong.

33

There's a sight you don't see every day—a swarm of worms flying across the Manhattan skyline. There were so many they darkened the sky. By squinting, I could see more worms rising from the ground to join the swarm, not only in the city but from as far away as New Jersey. At the center of the flying worm-storm stood the robed Queen of Worms, her body shining blue like a glowworm. Floating alongside her, Matoka was perched on a writhing ledge.

This had to be the most impressive jailbreak I'd ever heard of.

As the Queen approached, Dr. Dendrite's robotic ape was landing a dozen blows for every one Junior did, but at a fraction of its height and mass, it was sorely outmatched by the scaly Old One. That didn't stop Chimpazoid from inflicting serious damage. It looked like Dr. D had broken the giant monster's fibula.

Junior hadn't wiped us out of the harbor yet because his attention was split and not just between his attackers. The gargantuan creature of darkness kept glancing back at the Statue of Liberty while at the same time trying to make it look like he wasn't. Not unlike certain a teenage Deep One who kept staring at my cleavage while he was begging for my help.

That was his weakness. When he took on the aspects of Isaac, he got them all—the good, the bad, and the horny.

I knew how to get Junior away from the city.

The broken bone was enough to make Junior focus on the fight long enough to grab Chimpazoid around the waist with his twitching left hand and tear off a robotic arm with his right. The giant sea monster smashed Chimpazoid over the head with the arm as if he was playing whack-a-mole. In between bashing, doggy Dendrite ejected from the head wearing a smaller but similar jetpack to the one I had on.

Dagon Junior turned his focus towards the lesser threats and swatted at the Mano with his right hand like they were rats. His left arm still wasn't moving well. The shark people all dove into the air then landed in the water below. More than a few looked stunned by the several story impact, but they still managed to swim away without Dagon Junior getting his claws on them. Next, Junior swung at his own neck but Shrill was faster and the mechanical lawyer scooped up her ogre husband and flew them both out of range.

Dagon Junior limped toward Battery Park and stepped out of the water onto the grass. Before his other foot could make landfall, the worm-storm enveloped him. Matoka leapt off her worm platform and I flew down by her.

The swarm of invertebrates congealed into one colossal form, which, while taller than Chimpazoid, barely reached past Dagon Junior's stomach.

The ground beneath the Queen of Worms erupted like a geyser hose, only instead of water, it was a gigantic stream of worms.

I waved doggy Dendrite towards me. When the eruption ended, the Queen of Worms was as tall as Junior and still in her orange jumpsuit and ragged black hooded cloak which had somehow expanded to fit her new gargantuan form.

The colossal Queen's "hands" oozed a stream of worms until she held Dagon Junior's right hand and wrist and his left shoulder. She matched Junior's strength and stopped him in his tracks.

"Sorry, Bikini. I did my best to hold him," Dendrite said, hovering beside me.

"You did amazing, Doctor…" I almost slipped and used his real name. "..Cuddles, I need your help." I turned to the shark woman. "Yours too, Matoka."

As Dagon Junior used the remains of Chimpazoid to bash in the head of the Queen of Worms, I told them my plan and why it needed both of them to work.

To their credit, each agreed.

"I wouldn't have to build it from scratch. I have just what you need. There's only one catch," doggy Dendrite said.

I'm ashamed to admit it but my first thought was that he was going to use the opportunity to extort something from me. After all, that's how we've spent the last few years before he retired from being a supervillain to build his rather odd relationship with his daughter.

My fears were unfounded.

"I used it to hide Chimpazoid in plain sight, including from those government idiots who wanted to scrap him. It's still in the cockpit in the head of the ape." Which was being used as a club by Junior with his good arm. "But I don't think I can make it in there and get out."

"I can," I said with more confidence than I felt.

"I'll help you," said Matoka.

"Absolutely, after I retrieve the device," I said.

"I meant I'd get the device," the shark woman said.

I shook my head. "Even wearing my jetpack, I'm smaller than you which means I have a better chance of fitting in the tiny cockpit and I'm less likely to attract Junior's attention up there. The last thing we need is his attention focused on one of us little people."

I whispered my plan to the worm I now wore as a ring and asked the Queen of Worms if she could kindly keep Junior distracted a little longer. Battling with a more powerful Old One must have been straining even her not inconsiderable power because instead of humming her answer, the end of the ring simply nodded. I took flight at water level alongside the clashing titans and circled behind Dagon Junior, hopefully out of his line of sight.

Old Ones often didn't need to see something to know it was happening, but I was counting on his wrestling match with the Queen of Worms to keep him from noticing me. The fact that he was new to having a physical form probably wouldn't hurt my chances either.

Rather than come up at head level where he might hear my jetpack, I came around his waist just below his right elbow. The Queen of Worms shifted her mass to try to hold his right arm still.

When Dendrite ejected, it left a small opening in the top of the Chimpazoid's head. The opening had been made even smaller by the repeated smashings. It was a good thing Matoka hadn't come with me. The shark woman never would've fit.

I was going to have to leave my jetpack behind to fit. It had a hover mode but having it stay anywhere near this battle of behemoths was a bad idea so I was going to use my watch to fly it above the clash and hover out of harm's way.

I slipped out of the straps and leapt onto the mechanical ape's head just as Dagon Junior's arm broke free of the Queen's wormy grip, smashing my jetpack and sending it tumbling towards the river below.

I used the momentum of the swinging arm to fall into the cockpit. It made me remember another twisted and darker villain who make a giant mech of his own and took the name of the control room a little too seriously.

Junior must've gotten his arm free entirely because Chimpazoid was being swung like a baseball bat causing me to do a very poor imitation of a pinball. After a nasty and painful ricochet, I grabbed hold of the seat straps. It would've been nice if I could have dropped myself in the pilot's chair but Dendrite had built it to hold his doggy form which was significantly smaller and canine.

Wrapping the strap around my arm stopped me from ricocheting around the cockpit. Instead, I was dangling like a piñata in a tornado, trying to avoid hitting the floor or ceiling.

The movement slowed to just a slow rocking—I imagined the Queen of Worms had regained her grip on Junior's arm. I was dangling off the side of the chair—down toward the right wall instead of the floor—and managed to not only get my hands on the device I came for but twist it out of its place on the control panel. It took me a second longer than it needed to as Dr. Dendrite had designed it to be the opposite of the traditional righty-tighty lefty-Lucy.

Still dangling, I twisted toward the blown hatch which was now in front of me instead of above. I swung my legs back and forth to build enough momentum and flung myself toward the only available exit.

I picked the wrong time to let go as Chimpazoid started falling. Junior must've lost his grip on the mech ape because it was plummeting. Instead of flying out, I was thrown into a wall. Fortunately, my zero-gravity training kicked in and I reached out to grab hold of the seatbelts and pull myself toward the pilot's chair. I'd never fit all of me so I strapped my legs in an instant before Chimpazoid smashed into the river.

34

Under normal circumstances, the impact should have killed me but I was counting on the fact that Dr. Dendrite was overly paranoid about protecting his brain no matter what form he was in. Dr. D didn't disappoint. The entire cabin was flooded by impact foam that shot out of the chair and enveloped me. It was better than airbags. When the mech hit the water, I was battered but alive.

The beautiful thing about impact foam is it absorbs force and a few seconds later becomes hard and inert and is easy to crack apart from the inside. Sadly, I wouldn't be alive for much longer as water from the Hudson River was pouring in through the blown escape hatch. With some other villain's handiwork, I would have been concerned about electrocution, but I knew Dr. Dendrite would've insulated everything to protect himself.

As much as I wanted to leave, it wasn't an option at the moment with the river water's rushing in through the opening. There is no way I could fight my way past that current so with the impact foam still holding me in place, I started deep breathing exercises to saturate my lungs with oxygen as the cabin filled with water. Once it filled, the pressure inside and out would be more or less equalized so I could swim out the hole.

In my training from both the Clown Ninja Monks and Henrietta Houdini, I've learned various ways to improve the time I could hold my breath. My best time is eight minutes and fifty-seven seconds but that was during a training exercise. Realistically, in this situation where my heart was pounding and physical exertion was necessary, I figured I had five, maybe six minutes tops before I passed out and drowned.

I broke apart all the foam above my waist then stripped off my bikini top and used it to strap the device I'd come for to my arm. I focused on the replacement bikini to make it useful.

I waited until my nose was brushing metal to take my last deep breath. I broke apart the last of the impact foam and moved toward the escape hatch.

My new bikini materialized as I was almost to the open hatch. This suit was made out of a type of aerogel created at the Helsinki University of Technology that is so buoyant that one pound of it can carry about a thousand pounds of cargo and it contains nanofibrils that have a lot of similarities with cellulose in plants. I had to fight to make my way down in the water far enough to get out the escape hatch, but once I was out, my bikini pulled me towards the surface. I just had to kick to get me to fresh air faster.

It wasn't until my head broke the water that I calmed down enough to be skeeved out by the fact that I was swimming in the Hudson River without a wet suit, goggles, or breathing mask.

The giant scaly leg nearest me lifted out of the water and hovered above me. Besides the fact that Dagon Junior had spotted me and was about to stomp me like a bug, I noticed two other things. His broken fibula was almost healed and there was a huge shark fin above the water headed towards me.

The fin dove beneath the water and something grabbed me around the waist. I was yanked so fast that it made riding a jet ski seem like standing still.

Even at that speed, the stomping foot still almost got us and the wake from the impact capsized a couple of ferries.

My ride didn't stop until we were a long way away from the struggle of the giants which is when Matoka's head popped above water.

"Thanks for the lift."

"I should get a job as a water taxi, pulling around people in a tiny boat," the shark woman said.

"In New York, people would pay for that," I said.

Doggy Dendrite dove out of the sky and used his jetpack to hover above us.

Without a word, two robotic hands extended from compartments on his dog collar and he reached into my bikini pouch and pulled out what I had retrieved—a masker, a holographic device that can make something look like something else. The mechanical arms fiddled with the controls and then pointed it at the Statue of Liberty. Light beams shot out and scanned Lady Liberty from crown to toes.

Doggy Dendrite made some more adjustments then a robotic hand gave the masker back to me. "It's all set."

Still treading water, I turned to the shark woman. "You still okay with this? Junior there could be a lot faster than you are."

"Fat chance." The shark woman looked up at the hovering dog with the human brain. "Let's do this."

A mechanical hand retracted into his color and emerged with a silvery roll of a familiar substance from the folded space inside his collar. Not unlike a famous police box, the collar was bigger on the inside.

"Duct tape? Really?" I said. "A scientist of your caliber uses duct tape?"

The dog with the human brain gave a hybrid of a chuckle and a bark. "Amazingly useful, particularly in a crisis." The furry scientist turned to the shark woman as she bobbed next to me in the river. "With your permission, Ms. Matoka, I'd like to attach the masker device to your back. Your dorsal fin would be the most effective spot."

The shark woman frowned and I heard a small rumble somewhere in the neighborhood of her throat, but she nodded and said, "Do what you must, Cuddles."

The shark woman floated on her belly as the flying dog use his collar's mechanical hands to secure the holographic masker.

"The hologram will have its center far above you, Ms. Matoka, but it will follow you wherever you go." Doggy Dendrite looked at me. "May I, Bikini?"

I nodded and floated on my back so the mechanical arms could put wire-thin bracelets on my wrists, ankles, and neck.

"With these, you'll control the body movements the hologram makes." A mechanical finger tapped the center of the coffee cup size device duct-taped to the shark woman's dorsal fin and a full-sized holographic replica of the Statue of Liberty appeared above us.

"Don't swim too fast. We don't want you losing him," I said.

"He may be faster than me. You don't want me to go too fast. You really should make up your mind, Bikini Jones." Matoka's voice sounded serious, but I believe she was making a joke. She took off swimming and the lifelike holographic replica kept pace with her.

Doggie Dendrite's hands again disappeared into his collar and out came the transparent pouch that held the sacrificial knife and the page from the Necronomicon. "I believe you'll be needing these."

I took them with a smile. "You were following behind me to save me if I needed it, weren't you?"

The dog shrugged. "Harper would be upset if anything

happened to you. You are her hero, you know."

Dr. Dendrite really had changed. It was still unsettling. "Thanks."

The dog with the human brain nodded. "May I offer you a lift?"

A glance showed that *The Brass Ring* was helping evacuate civilians.

"Sure."

Mechanical hands reached into the water and grasped me under my armpits. The two of us shot up into the air.

"Junior hasn't noticed our bait yet," I said.

"I have this," doggy Dendrite said. A moment later incredibly loud voice boomed from his collar. "Hey fish face! Look behind you. I think she likes you."

Creatures of the darkness have the ability to learn languages quickly, but Junior would have absorbed Isaac's understanding of English instantly. Still grappling with the millions of worms blocking his path, Dagon Junior turned his scaly head. I mimicked a sultry finger wiggle as best I could dangling a hundred feet in the air. Holographic Miss Liberty mimicked me and Junior froze and stared, his eyes wide.

For the first time, I got a good look at the hologram and realized didn't look exactly like the original.

"Did you make her chest bigger? And her skirt shorter?" I asked.

"I did, plus narrowed her waist and made her hips and buttocks more rounded as well as her hair longer and more flowing," doggy Dendrite said. "And her robes more revealing. And I got rid of the crown and the torch."

"Why?"

"You hypothesize that this Old One has absorbed the qualities of his teenage host. As you're hoping to use his libido to lead him away, I thought it best to make the statue's appearance more appealing to a teenage boy. Although I suspect her color being a similar shade to his skin doesn't hurt matters at all. Also, with all the trouble you are having with people trying to cancel you, I figured the last thing you needed was people accusing you of desecrating Lady Liberty so I created Miss Libby."

Reluctantly, I nodded my head. "Good plan."

"Obviously. Mega-genius, remember?"

He was doing amazing, so I let him have it. "I do."

With a massive push, Dagon Junior shoved the Queen of Worms from him and turned to face our Miss Libby.

I brought my hand up to my lips and blew him a kiss followed by a tiny delicate wave and beckoning motion with my index finger.

Suddenly we were off to the races. Dagon Junior bounded through the water straight at the hologram. It took the better part of a second for Matoka to react and swim faster toward open waters. The hologram turned her back towards Junior and went on autopilot. I was impressed with the artistry in how her hourglass shape wiggled her hips side to side as if she was some siren in a red dress in an old PI movie.

Junior was clocking some serious speed and it was once again obvious that the holographic Libby was very much to his liking.

Despite Matoka's bravado, the gargantuan creature of darkness was not only keeping pace with the shark woman but slowly closing the gap between them. I doubted we had more than a few minutes before Junior caught up to Libby. I suspected he was going to be rather upset when she found out how insubstantial their budding relationship truly was.

Seconds away from the open ocean, Junior was far enough away from the city for me to start the next phase of my plan. I took out the contents of the transparent pouch and began chanting in ancient Samarian. Trust me, if you are going to fight things of ancient darkness, learning the basics of the language is a necessity.

I pressed the knife against the page and rubbed off a drop of Isaac's drying blood that was still on the blade, then chanted louder. The floating portal to the dark dimension that was still near the docks shifted a few feet in my direction.

"I'm too far away. My chanting isn't loud enough."

"Is that all?" Doggy Dendrite said. A third mechanical arm appeared holding a microphone in front of my mouth.

"You just happen to have a microphone?" I said.

"Harper likes karaoke."

I resumed chanting, but this time my words made the glass in the nearby skyscrapers vibrate as my voice reverberated from where the broken Chimpazoid lay beneath the water on the riverbed.

The portal took off straight at us like it was a flying saucer.

I stopped chanting long enough to yell, "Fly! We need to get it above Junior!"

Doggy Dendrite's jetpack went into overdrive and the race was on for us to catch up with Junior before he caught up with Matoka and the portal caught up with any of us. I suppose we also resembled what it might look like if the Thanksgiving Day Parade was ever held on water but I didn't think even Santa Claus was going to be able to save us this time, even if he did owe me. Besides, he's probably still too broken up about what happened when we saved an alien world's Christmas with the help of Snazzy, my sister's childhood Teddy bear. There are no words to describe what that shameless hussy, the former Mrs. Claus, did to Santa.

But she got what she deserved.

The worm on my finger screamed. I looked back and saw that the vortex was sucking in worms, pulling apart the Queen's form.

The portal could take the Queen of Worms from this world back to the dark dimension where she'd never be able to hurt anyone, but she's shown that she's changed. Before I beat her the first time, she helped a teenager and allowed herself to be imprisoned rather than hurting him. Now she's come to my aid against a more powerful Old One. I know plenty of people who would let her be reclaimed by the darkness to make sure she never turns on humanity. I can't stand seeing someone be punished because of a good deed.

Stopping my chanting, I screamed, "Take us higher!" My voice still was coming from beneath the water.

Doggy Dendrite looked back and saw that the vortex was making like a vacuum cleaner trying to suck up all the fish bait in the freezer.

Being the practical kind, he looked at me questioningly. I nodded.

We kept gaining altitude until Junior looked about the size of a Barbie doll. Behind us, worms stopped being sucked into the dark dimension. The worm ring on my finger stopped screaming and hummed, "Thank you."

I resumed chanting. Our altitude might work to our advantage, even if it allowed the portal to gain on us. If we dove just right, we could come in above Junior, so hopefully, he wouldn't notice the vortex until it was too late. As Dendrite had just bragged again about how he was a mega-genius and understood things that others could not, so I didn't bother to tell him what I wanted him to do and instead just pointed down at Junior, then moved my hand at the angle I was thinking.

To his credit, Dendrite realized exactly what I wanted and we dove at that angle using the pull of gravity to increase our speed so we shot above Dragon Junior's head so we were between him and the holographic Libby. He was seconds away from catching her.

I pointed again towards Matoka, who was swimming along the surface at the center of the hologram again. Dendrite knew what I was thinking. We dove and a fourth appendage shot out with a blade on the end. With surgical precision, it sliced through the duct tape around the masker, grabbed the holographic projector and we took off into the sky. Matoka was smart enough to swim off to the side and Junior watched as the object of his affections rose out of the ocean and into the sky. We kept moving forward until the portal was above Junior. I ceased my chanting and the portal stopped moving.

I started a new chant and the portal changed color and inky tentacles reached through from the darkness, hungry for any taste of life.

The closest thing to life in their reach was Dagon Junior and the tentacles latched onto him. Junior in turn tried to latch onto us. Dendrite performed evasive maneuvers but the mad scientist wasn't fast enough and the leviathan latched onto my ankle, caught between the tips of his colossal fingers.

Dendrite revved his jetpack up to the maximum to try to pull me free, but Junior had too good a grip on my ankle. No sense in both of us dying, so I did some squirming of my own and slid out from the metallic hands holding my armpits.

Doggy Dendrite shot away into the sky much as someone would if they were playing tug-of-war when the other side let go of the rope.

Dagon Junior was bellowing as the tentacles pulled and the vortex sucked him back towards the dark dimension.

As mighty as his struggle was, he was barely holding his own. Junior wasn't powerful enough to pull away. The spawn of Dagon dangled me upside down in front of his mouth. I was hit with breath that smelled worse than a thousand dead fish. The effort it took to roar his anger at me moved him a few feet closer to being dragged home against his will. More tentacles reached out, figuring since they weren't going to be getting out the least they could do was ruin it for him. Not a lot of kindness or comradery in the dark dimension.

Junior decided he wasn't going back alone and moved me closer to his mouth in an attempt to eat me.

I was almost two hundred feet in the air so there was a decent chance the fall might kill me, but those jaws and teeth definitely would. I did a sit-up and stabbed Junior's index finger with the sacrificial blade I was still holding. The Old One recoiled at the touch, letting go of me. As I plummeted, I twisted and tossed the dagger right towards his remaining pupil and got a bullseye. Despite being relatively splinter-sized, it'd been part of what summoned him and was one of the few things on Earth that could hurt Junior.

Blinding pain caused him to lash out in rage and stop resisting the pull of the portal. Junior shot up into the air where more tentacles of his friends and neighbors grabbed hold and pulled him in quicker than I was falling. There were several ways I could close the portal but there was no way of saving poor Isaac. I bit my tongue and spit blood on the page of the Necronomicon still in my hand. I let go and it was sucked towards the portal. I chanted some more ancient Sumerian and the portal became to shrink and close. It was a race to see if the dark dimension would reclaim all of him before the portal closed. The page of the Necronomicon slipped through and as the source of the summoning, that closed the portal entirely, but not all of Junior made it through. The closure chopped off the creature's big toe.

We were again cut off from the dark dimension. At least until someone else was stupid enough to invite in something that hated all life when the next alignment came around.

The sucking portal had exerted some force slowing my fall, but now that it was gone, I plummeted. I turned and positioned my body like I learned when I fought vampire cliff divers in Acapulco.

I hit the water just right so that I broke the surface and not all the bones in my body.

I still went deep. I was exhausted and struggled to swim toward the surface, but if it wasn't for the buoyancy of my aerogel bikini, I don't think I would've made it.

Magic takes a lot out of someone who hasn't dedicated their life to training. As soon as I broke the surface, I rolled over on my back and promptly passed out.

35

When I woke up—after the usual inner jubilation that once again I was somehow still alive—there was a lot of aftermath to cleanup.

Happily, with the help of Stanley and Hany, the bureaucratic aspects didn't take too long.

The Church of the Majestic Deep was another matter. Turns out most of the membership was a tad unhappy about me sending the son of their god back to the dark dimension and decided to do something about it.

Forty Deep Ones with automatic weapons arrived en mass in white church vans at Bikini Tower.

Once on the sidewalk, they got into a marching formation and approached the building.

I met them before they could get close. No reason for any innocents to get hurt if these religious nut jobs started shooting.

"Can I help you, gentlemen?" I said. The four who helped me clean and the six at Castle Clinton weren't among them.

"You've done enough, stopping the world from being made over in Dagon's image as the prophecy foretold," the one in charge shouted.

"That was trumped by it being foretold that Bikini Jones would kick Dagon Junior's scaly butt," I said.

"Foretold by who?"

"Me," I answered.

"And calling one of our god's butts scaly is racist," shouted another.

"Was his butt scaly?" I said.

"Well, yeah."

"What part of that is racist then?" I asked.

The Deep One stammered. "It just is."

"It's not even a little," I said. "I'm surprised you are all so worked up considering that your church head was going to let you all fend for yourselves and maybe die."

"Fake news! Braham Leviticus would never betray us!" the

leader shouted.

"You've seen the footage, right?" The people who hung around to record were foolish, but their videos were coming in handy.

"Deep fakes."

"They are not. I was there," I said.

The leader brought his AR-15 up and pointed it at me. The rest did the same. "And soon you won't be anywhere."

"Gentlemen, I trust you aren't bothering my favorite cousin." From behind the armed cultists came a voice as deep as the ocean.

I smiled. My sister Betty Lou hated when he said that.

"Listen, buddy, any of us is ten times stronger than you," the Deep One leader said without turning around. An exaggeration of their strength advantage over a human but not too much of one. "Your cousin is as good as dead, so give us a minute and you can hang around and bury her."

"Hurt a hair on her head and I won't leave enough of you to be buried at sea," my cousin said.

The leader rolled his eyes and spun around, fully intending to shoot whoever was behind him. The sight of the tentacled face made him freeze mid-turn.

"Cthulhu Jones?" he stammered.

"In the handsome green flesh," CJ said, reaching out for the AR-15. "May I?"

The Deep One nodded rapidly. "Sure."

Cthulhu Jones was strong, ridiculously so. Deep Ones looked like wimps in comparison.

"I've never been a fan of guns," CJ said.

"Me neither," agreed the trembling Deep One.

"Really? So what's with all the automatic weapons then?"

"Protection."

"I only see people who need protection from you." Cthulhu Jones bent the barrel of the gun back and tied it in a knot. "I'd feel a lot more comfortable if you would all put the safeties on…" My cousin turned to me. "Bikini, do these guns…"

"AR-15s," I said.

"… have safeties?"

I nodded. "It's a small cylinder above the trigger."

"Thanks, cuz." CJ turned back to the heavily armed Deep Ones. "Put on your safeties and place your guns in a pile in front of me for our buy-back program."

"These cost us over a grand each. What are you giving us in exchange?" shouted one Deep One from the back of the crowd.

"The opportunity to walk away under your own power," CJ said.

"Guys, why are we taking crap from octopus face here? There are forty of us and one of him," the same guy in the back said.

"Shaddup!" the leader shouted. "Cthulhu Jones is the son of Cthulhu."

"He can't be," the guy in the back whispered.

"That's what my dad said until the paternity test came back," CJ said. "Now since my dad and the guy you worship were pals back in the day, I'm willing to forget about this as long as my cousin Bikini is."

He looked at me. "I'll consider it under the right circumstances."

"Good point. You will all leave your guns and never trouble Bikini Jones again. Oh, and turn over any bits or pieces of the Necronomicon that might be lying around any of your churches or properties."

The guy in the back had just the right mix of bravado and stupidity to speak up again. "And what if we don't?"

CJ stepped forward and the crowd parted for him until he reached the heckler. He just stood and stared the amphibiman in the eyes. The heckler stared back, then trembled. Seconds later, the heckler collapsed screaming and convulsing.

"Anyone else want to suggest not listening?"

There was a sea of shaking heads.

"Now pile 'em up and apologize to my cousin Bikini," CJ ordered.

The automatic weapons were laid on the sidewalk and I got thirty-nine apologies.

The Deep Ones picked up their fallen member, got in their white vans, and sped off.

"Thanks for stepping in—" I had preparations in place but CJ did a better job of it than I could have. "—but did you really have to do the Abyss stare?"

CJ shrugged. "I didn't do anything much. Besides that particular glimpse doesn't affect decent folks. He saw the tiniest bit of true darkness and recognized he had invited some inside himself by his thoughts and actions. That realization gave him a panic attack. Don't worry about him. He'll be up and about in a few days and may even be a better person if he learns that he can cast out the darkness the same way he invited it in—by his thoughts and actions."

Despite the horrors my cousin has lived through, he has a good heart.

"I figured one panic attack was a better option than a mass shooting," CJ said.

I nodded and hugged my cousin. He hugged me back with his arms and tentacles. It's not as creepy as it sounds. When we were kids, he explained that they were like tiny arms but whenever he touched someone with them, they freaked out. I held out my hand and let him touch my fingers. After that, it was no big deal for either of us.

"Did you catch the wendigo who was killing the golfers?"

"Turns out there was a wendigo but she was in a twelve-step program and hadn't killed or eaten human flesh in years. The actual killer was a Blemmye."

"Those little guys with no head and their face in their chest?" I said.

"Yep. It had been driven out of its home in the Mojave Desert by land developers and relocated to a sand trap on the golf course. One of the golfers hit it with a golf ball, then tried to play it where it landed and was killed and eaten. Things escalated from there. But I caught it and they finished the golf tournament."

"How'd you do?"

"Came in second. Might have taken first if I didn't use a shot on the last hole to knock out the Blemmye before he could eat the front runner. It turns out, I like golf. Go figure," CJ said with a laugh. "I'm sorry I missed the summoning, but it seems like you managed okay."

"With a lot of help from my friends," I admitted.

"That's what friends are for," CJ said. "Doesn't mean you can't thank them."

"I was planning on it. And you're invited too."

36

My cousin was right. Just saying thank you—which I did—didn't seem anywhere near enough for facing off against an Old One so I made a phone call and rented out the Tommy Gunners Bar and Thrill for an early dinner a few hours before their regular showtime.

I have to confess to being more than a little shocked when Joey Capone offered to do it gratis as he put it. Said us saving New York saved the restaurant and feeding the folks who did the saving was the least they could do. I appreciated the sentiment. While the restaurant may have been off to a strong start—the early reviews from the papers, magazines, and bloggers had helped generate a lot of word-of-mouth—it was still far too early life for such a new business to be giving away that much food for free not to mention absorbing the wages of the staff, so I insisted that dinner was on me and invited everyone who had helped. I insisted there be no show. Everyone coming would be more than able to entertain themselves.

Sherman brought his lovely wife and the cyborg octogenarian was giving Big Lug tips on being the doorman for the restaurant. Lug pointed out that he was more of a host/bouncer to which Sherman countered that every doorman at some point is called upon to execute the same role as a bouncer.

I doubted such services would be needed tonight. The group was battered and bruised, some more than others, but all of them were very much alive and would be as good as new after some rest.

Shrill and Crunch were adorable. Despite the huge mismatch in size, they had their arms intertwined each around the other while sipping champagne. Next to them, Hany and Stanley clinked glasses.

Dr. Dendrite and his daughter Harper were busy talking with Jenny. The alien with the human brain had become rather partial to the former mad scientist ever since he saved her life by surgically giving her control of her alien body.

Tapedo and most of the shark people were over in the corner, slicing chunks off of a rotisserie cow. A few were still back watching out for the children who were responding remarkably well to the treatment and given a few months would be back to normal. Before you get overly impressed by what they were dining on, the Bar and Thrill does not have the facilities needed to cook an entire cow. I modified one of my blasters so it could cook the meat.

Matoka and the Queen of Worms were at the bar putting down shots.

The Mayor sat next to them, sipping a beer and trying his best to act like he wasn't extremely nervous or the tiniest bit terrified.

"Bikini, you must drink with us!" Matoka shouted. I joined them and the shark woman slapped me on the shoulder. I was impressed that I managed to not be knocked down by the comradery blow.

Antonio poured us each a shot. The three of us clinked glasses and downed our drinks. Neither commented that I wasn't drinking alcohol. Unlike the two of them, I could get drunk. Because of Matoka's size, it would probably take a barrel of whiskey to do the job. While worms could get drunk, I wasn't sure the Queen could. It would probably take a tremendous amount of alcohol before she even felt tipsy. I was glad I negotiated the alcohol at cost.

"I must thank you," the shark woman bellowed. "Not only are you the savior of the shark people, but you came to my aid after I behaved so badly to this gentleman." Matoka rather gently slapped the mayor on the back. It took him about a half-second longer than usual to smile. "I am so glad to not have to return to Rikers Island."

"I was happy to do it," I said.

"Me too," said the mayor. "The least we could do after you helped save Manhattan."

The mayor had helped, but I still had to burn through a lot of favors to keep both of the ladies from going back to jail. The mayor was easy to convince, but the Manhattan District Attorney was tougher. She was running for re-election on a tough-on-crime platform.

"Thank you from me as well. I was tired of that tiny prison as well," vibrated the swirling mass that took the place of a throat. The Queen of Worms still wore a black hooded robe, but her orange jumpsuit was gone. It had been replaced by a long dress that looked very much like it was red satin. It was a bit jarring at first but I liked it.

"I explained that you broke out at *my* request." Yes, I took full responsibility for the jailbreak. And rightly so. They only broke out because I asked for help. Technically, I only asked the Queen of Worms for help. Matoka volunteered on her own. "The fact that you both surrendered yourselves back into custody helped convinced the DA that you both had turned over a new leaf."

Since Matoka hadn't gone to trial or been convicted yet, the DA was willing to drop the charges.

The Queen of Worms situation was a tad more complicated.

"So now I have undisputed freedom and my crimes are forgotten because the governor of New York excused my behavior?"

"Pardoned. It doesn't mean what you did is forgotten. The governor has just agreed to not continue punishment."

The governor needed some convincing, so I showed the governor some of the internet footage of the Queen fighting Dagon Junior then pointed out that she was only in the prison because she was allowing it and out of respect for me. I asked him what was going to happen one day if she tired of being at Rikers and decided to leave. How would the corrections officers with a handful of gadgets stop someone as powerful as the Queen of Worms?

He was receptive when I pointed out that a pardon would buy the state some goodwill from the Queen but I had to personally vouch for her. It didn't hurt that I made her another offer.

"I thank you for the job," the Queen said with a slight nod.

"You're welcome. I'm thrilled you accepted," I said.

That's right, the Queen of Worms will be working for the Bikini Foundation.

Now not only will we have renewable seeds shipping out throughout the world, but we will have help making sure they can grow. There are plenty of areas where the soil is less than optimal for farming. The Queen's abilities to control worms mixed with her innate power meant she could change the composition of soil and allow crops to grow in regions where they would've had great difficulty previously.

With any luck, we may be able to nip future famines in the bud and make sure thousands, maybe millions of people have enough food. Some shipments were going into war-torn countries where warlords might try to hijack the shipments. By having the Queen of Worms accompany the seeds, I predict no one is going to be stupid enough to interfere with us providing crops for the hungry.

"I can't believe that you also got me a job among humans," Matoka said. "What's even more unbelievable is that I agreed to it."

"It's right up your stream," I said.

After firing Chief Flag based on video footage of my arrest and interrogation, plus the preliminary evidence of his taking bribes from Leviticus, the mayor asked me what it would take for me not to sue the city. I told him dropping all charges against Matoka and hiring her for the NYPD Harbor Patrol would go a long way toward avoiding a lawsuit.

He agreed and gave her a special dispensation to begin work even before she goes through the police academy. She worked for an entire shift today and found six guns that had been tossed in the Hudson. Matoka would be performing regular patrols to check for explosives on bridges and help prevent any smuggling or drugs from slipping through. If she did well, the mayor was open to considering hiring other shark people.

"I think you'll make a fine police officer," the mayor said. "Although I have no idea where they'll find a uniform in your size." There were some chuckles at that. "But don't you worry about that. I'll make sure it's taken care of. Now that you're on the job, Officer Matoka, New York's waterways will be the safest they've ever been."

I suspect she will get a lot of practice working crowd control too. People are scared of sharks in the water, but the idea of one that can walk up to you on land could be downright terrifying. People will think three times before causing trouble in front of the shark woman. Plus, now that she was a police officer, she could help collect evidence about the dumping near the shark people's home and prevent it from happening again.

Shrill and Crunch had convinced the judge to freeze Voxamatik's assets so they would be able to pay for the cleanup. CEO Kalvin Lackthorne had been arrested not just on illegal dumping charges, but by the fact that his primary stockholder—Reverend Braham Leviticus—was the instigator of this whole mess and had masterminded the scheme to get rid of the shark people. He didn't want the Deep Ones to have any water-based competition or any interference during the rising of Dagon Junior.

Mrs. and Reverend Leviticus were in custody. Turns out his AR-15 wielding cultists who overheard his true intentions beat him to within a few millimeters of his life, but Deep Ones are resilient, so he survived albeit much the worse for wear.

You'd be surprised how hard it is to prove and prosecute someone for summoning an otherworldly entity to take over and destroy the world. That case was going to take a little while to build. The more immediate arrest was for the attempted murder of his son.

That's right, I said attempted. I figured the horndog was lost since most of Dagon's body went back through the portal to the dark dimension. Turns out the toe that he left behind was crucial to Isaac's survival. Matoka swam me to shore while Dr. Dendrite used his jetpack to tow the toe to shore. You can take the scientist out of the mad, but not the mad out of the scientist. Dendrite wanted to study the toe at great length, likely exploring the possibility of adapting the tissue into a new form should he ever want to transplant his brain again.

It turns out that Isaac's mind and soul climbed into the toe to not get sucked into the dark dimension. When it was amputated, the Queen of Worms could sense Isaac's presence. Manipulating the energies of her native dimension was second nature to her, so she was able to manipulate the flesh and mold it into a very reasonable facsimile of Isaac's original body. Although being who he is, Isaac asked for a few further adjustments, improving the size of his muscles and other body parts. The Queen of Worms obliged.

Isaac filed charges and swore out a complaint against his parents, which was backed up by the footage of a tourist who had not left Castle Clinton and live-streamed the sacrifice while hiding inside the castle. Since the video showed Leviticus slicing open his son, it shouldn't be hard to make the attempted murder charge stick.

At the moment, Isaac was trying to chat up Shrill.

Although her programming extended to more forms of pleasure than just the physical, the mechanical woman's body had been designed with a male libido in mind and the horndog was stupid enough to try to pick up the married android. I watched in amusement as Crunch returned from the bar and slowly stepped up behind him and blocked much of the surrounding light. The horndog Deep One turned his head slowly, backing up when he looked into the frowning face of the ogre, who for effect was allowing his lower teeth to jut out over his upper lip. The lawyer then reached up to straighten his tie but the movement of his enormous arm was enough to make the teenager dive for cover, fearing that it was a blow meant for him.

The ogre made a dismissive and sweeping broom-like gesture with the forefingers of his hand which caused the Deep One to bolt away to hide behind his sister. Lorraine was sitting at a table chatting with my cousin. Having grown up in a cult of sea monsters, Loraine was used to being around unusual-looking people, so Cthulhu Jones' appearance didn't faze her, which I think my cousin was enjoying. As much as people stare at my chest, it was far worse with folks staring at CJ's face tentacles.

And since she could get past CJ's appearance, she was able to see the big-hearted and funny guy he really is. In fact, I think she may have been developing a crush on him. My cousin can be oblivious to certain things, so I'd mention it later, so he didn't do something unintentional to hurt her feelings as she was way too young for him.

Miss Bootlegger ran out of her back room to bark at the Queen of Worms and the shark woman.

"Is this a snack before dinner?" Matoka said.

"Yum," the Queen of Worms said, a particularly large invertebrate coming out of where a human mouth would be and making a motion that mimicked the licking of lips. Big Lug ran over from the door, quite possibly the fastest I've ever seen the large, retired gangster move as he scooped up the puppy.

"You can't eat her."

Big Lug craned his neck back to stare up at someone even bigger than he was. As he took note of all her teeth, there was a slight trembling of his knees. Big Lug could mop the floor with most humans, but against Matoka he would likely end up as fish food.

"We can't?" Matoka said.

"Why not?" hummed the Queen of Worms. Maybe it was because I'd had more interactions with her, but I noticed a slight titter to the vibrations of her voice, her equivalent of a giggle. She was trying to be funny by messing with Big Lug. I wasn't exactly sure if Matoka was or wasn't.

"Because she's my dog and one of my bestest friends and I don't let nobody eat none of my friends." Big Lug's voice only quivered a little. Spats Magool and Joey Capone stepped up alongside Big Lug. Neither of them seemed exactly sure what they could do, but it didn't matter. They had Big Lug's back, even if he was dumb enough to get into it with a ten-foot-tall shark woman and a creature of primordial darkness.

"We'd be happy to get youse hors d'oeuvres but I'm afraid anything alive is simply not on our menu," Joey Capone said, as Antonio the moll rushed over and placed a pair of very large, barely cooked T-bones in front of the pair.

"That seems like an excellent policy," Matoka said.

"Standing up for one's friends is one of the few traits of humans that neither confuses nor disgusts me. It's very gracious of you to bring us snacks and allow us to visit your establishment," hummed the Queen of Worms as she placed what passed for her hands over her steak. Matoka simply swallowed hers whole, bone and all.

The worms over the steak oozed something that dissolved the meat to primordial goo, followed quickly by the bone. Oddly enough, eating the bone was not a feature of her dark nature. It came from the worms.

Some worms had the ability to eat and dissolve through bone. Others could excrete poison. The Old One was possibly one of the most dangerous beings on the planet. I was glad, for the moment at least, that not only was she on our side but on my payroll.

I realize I was wrong in assuming that Matoka has swallowed her whole steak. She'd torn off a small hunk which the shark woman offered to Miss Bootlegger. The gift of food was enough to make the dog stop barking and start wagging his tail. She ate it and even allowed Matoka to scratch her behind the ears with a finger that was as big as any of her doggie legs. I stepped away and went over to the Leviticus twins and my cousin.

"I have some good news."

"My pickle of the month crate arrived?" CJ said.

Loraine giggled and Isaac rolled his eyes.

"I meant for the twins," I said.

"You mean besides putting our parents in jail so they can't abuse us anymore?" Loraine said.

"Did they take the plea deal?" Isaac said, but he was staring at my cleavage again.

"Horndog, that's incredibly rude. When you talk to a woman,

look her in the eyes, not in the chest. Trust me, she will appreciate it."

Isaac had the decency to blush this time, although it was more of a darker green tint than red. "Sorry."

"If you're sorry, then stop doing it. My team found your aunt and uncle on your father's side. They left the cult a little after you two were born and if you ignore the green skin, scales, and yellow eyes of your uncle, they seem to be pretty typical middle-class Americans. When we told them what happened, they agreed to let you come live with them, which I figured would be a lot better than going to the foster care system."

Loraine was so happy and began gushing as she jumped up to hug me. "Thanks for everything, Bikini!"

Isaac moved in close, trying to get a hug as well. And I might very well have let him if he hadn't creepily licked his lips first. I stuck out my hand for him to shake it. Visibly disappointed, he did.

Aditte pulled me aside. "We just got a call from the NYPD."

"I guess we're back in their good graces again," I said.

"When someone live streams you saving the city and you get rid of a corrupt police Chief, that tends to happen. Anyway, pterodactyls are attacking people at Rockaway Beach. They've requested your assistance. Shall I let them know you're on your way, boss?" Aditte said.

"By the time we fight traffic back to Bikini Tower, I can be most of the way to Rockaway."

The mole woman smiled. "If only *The Brass Ring* was parked on top of the roof." Seeing my mouth open, Aditte correctly predicted what I was about to say. "Don't worry, it's in hover mode, not touching the building at all. And it's cloaked except for the air traffic safety blinking lights on the top."

Which was a good thing. You'd be surprised by how many things besides planes and helicopters are flying around New York that could crash into an invisible spaceship.

"Too bad my flight pack flight pack hit the drink," I said. Dr. Dendrite's was too small as it was geared to hold a small dog and Hany's was back at the Tower.

"True, although Matoka did fish it out of the Hudson for us. The lab techs say they should have it up and running in two or three weeks," Aditte said. "Which doesn't do you a lot of good now.

However, I do have your glider suit on board, which while not as fast or controllable as a jetpack still has propulsion units in the boots which would let you meet pterodactyls in their own environment."

"I guess I better go stop the pterodactyls."

"Did I hear pterodactyls? You want some help, cousin?" Cthulhu Jones said, coming up behind me.

"Sure, cousin," I said.

"You want me to ask anyone else to help?" Aditte said, motioning to the rest of the room with her furry chin.

"Nah. Let them enjoy the party. We got this."

There has long been a debate among certain obscure and drunken literary scholars about whether **PATRICK THOMAS** was raised by Cthulhu, a leprechaun in a Manhattan bar, or two human parents. What there is no arguing about is that Patrick is the award-winning author of 40 books including the beloved fantasy humor *Murphy's Lore series* (9 books from *Tales from Bulfinche's Pub* to *The Mug Life*), as well as 2 books in the future space adventures in the *Startenders* series.

The Murphy's Lore After Hours spin-offs star the half pixie/ogre Terrorbelle (*Fairy With A Gun, Fairy Rides The Lightning,* and *Terrorbelle The Unconquered*); the former demon-possessed serial killer Agent Karver of the Department of Mystic Affairs (*Dead To Rites, Rites of Passage*); the cursed magí Hex (*By Darkness Cursed* and *By Invocation Only*); Vince Argus, the Soul For Hire (*Greatest Hits*); and Negral, a forgotten Sumerian god who works as Hell's Detective (*Lore & Dysorder, Bullets & Brimstone,* and the graphic novel *The Moon Maniac* with Blair Webb).

His *Mystic Investigators* paranormal mystery series includes *Shadows & Brimstone* (omnibus of *Bullets & Brimstone* and *From The Shadows* with John L. French), *Once Upon In Crime* (omnibus of *Once More Upon A Time* and *Partners In Crime* with Diane Raetz) *Mystic Investigators,* and *Mean Streets. Assassins' Ball* is his first traditional mystery, co-written with John L. French. He co-edited *Camelot 13, New Blood, Hear Them Roar* and was an editor for the magazines *Fantastic Stories of the Imagination* and *Pirate Writings*.

His other works include the steampunk *As The Gears Turn.* the space epic *Exile & Entrance,* and the *Bikini Jones* series. Patrick's darkly humorous advice column *Dear Cthulhu* has been running since 2005 and has 6 collections including *Cthulhu Knows Best* and *What Would Cthulhu Do?* The Dear Cthulhu advice empire has expanded from magazines and books to radio as Dear Cthulhu now broadcasts monthly on the show Destinies: The Voice of Science Fiction which is hosted by Dr. Howard Margolin.

Over 100 of his stories have been published in magazines and anthologies. His noir novella appears in *Murder in Montague Falls.* A number of his books were part of the props department of the *CSI* television show and *Nightcaps* was even thrown at a suspect's head. His urban fantasy *Fairy With A Gun* had been optioned for film and TV by Laurence Fishburne's Cinema Gypsy Productions. Top Men Productions has turned his *Soul For Hire* Story, *Act of Contrition,* into a short film.

He also writes books for kids as PATRICK T. FIBBS including the YA *Emotional Support Nifghtmare,* the midde readers *Undead Kid Diaries: Over My Dead Body, the Babe B. Bear Mysteries: Bad Hair Day, Joy Reaper Checks Out,* the picture book *Fushcia The Mermaid Who Loved Pink,* and *the Ughabooz* picture books *5 Silly Monsters Jumping On The Zed* and *On Top Of A Yeti,* and the early reader *Soggy Goes to the Beach.*

Please drop by www.patthomas.net or follow him at I_PatrickThomas at Twitter or www.facebook.com/PatrickThomasAuthor to learn more.

Help is only
a Rainbow Away…

"Mix Gaiman's American Gods and Robinson's Callahan's Crosstime Saloon on Prachett's Discworld and you get an idea of Thomas' Murphy's Lore." -David Sherman, author o STARFIST and Demontech

"ENTERTAINING, INVENTIVE AND DELIGHTFULLY CREEPY." -JONATHAN MABERRY, New York Times and Bram Stoker Award Winning Author

"SLICK… ENTERTAINING Paul Di Filippo, ASIMOV'S

"HUMOR, OUTRAGEOUS ADVENTURES, & SOME CLEVER PLOT TWISTS." -Don D'Ammassa, SCIENC FICTION CHRONICLE

PATRICK THOMAS

DEAR CTHULHU
The advice column to END all advice columns

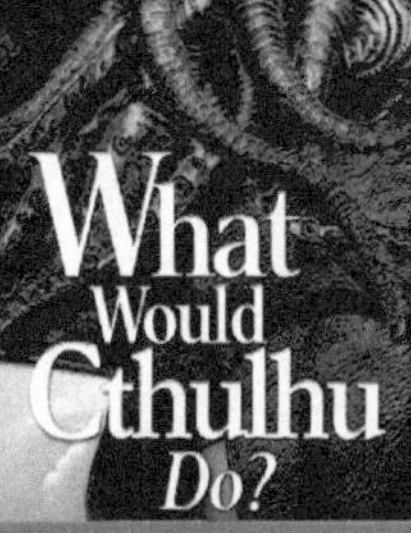

AVE Dark DAY
PATRICK THOMAS
GOOD ADVICE for BAD PEOPLE
PATRICK THOMAS
CTHULHU KNOWS BEST
PATRICK THOMAS
What Would Cthulhu Do?
PATRICK THOMAS
CTHULHU HAPPENS
PATRICK THOMAS
CTHULHU Explains It All
PATRICK THOMAS

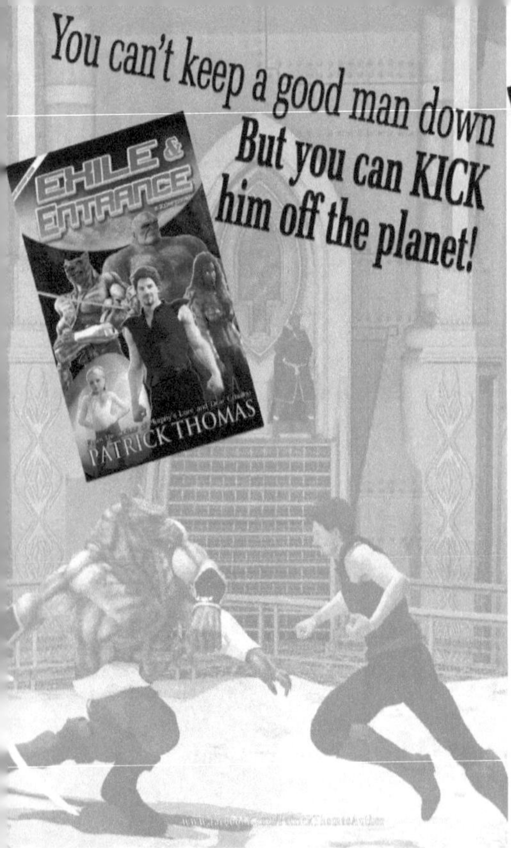
You can't keep a good man down
But you can KICK
him off the planet!
EXILE & ENTRANCE
PATRICK THOMAS

TALES OF STEAMWORLD
AS THE GEARS TURN
PATRICK THOMAS
Steampunk Mayhem from
the author of Murphy's Lore
& Dear Cthulhu!
Grin
'Em
WWW.PATTHOMAS.N
www.facebook.com/PatrickThomasAuthor

MURPHY'S LORE
"Delightfully Oddball"
-Dave Truesdale, SFSite
"Hilariously intelligent"
-Luke Reviews
STAR TENDERS
PATRICK THOMAS
CONSTELLATION PRIZE
PATRICK THOMAS
From behind
the bar
To Across
The STARS
Find us on Facebook!
From The Murphy's Lore Universe of
PATRICK THOMAS
WWW.PATTHOMAS.NET

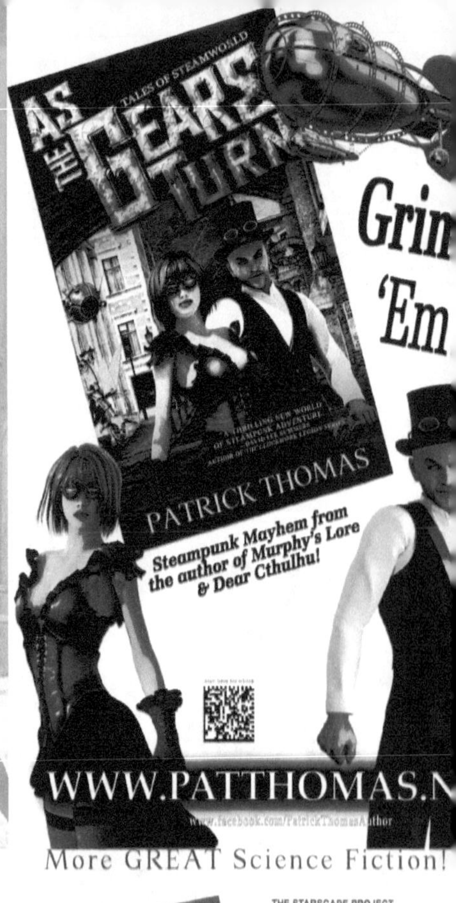

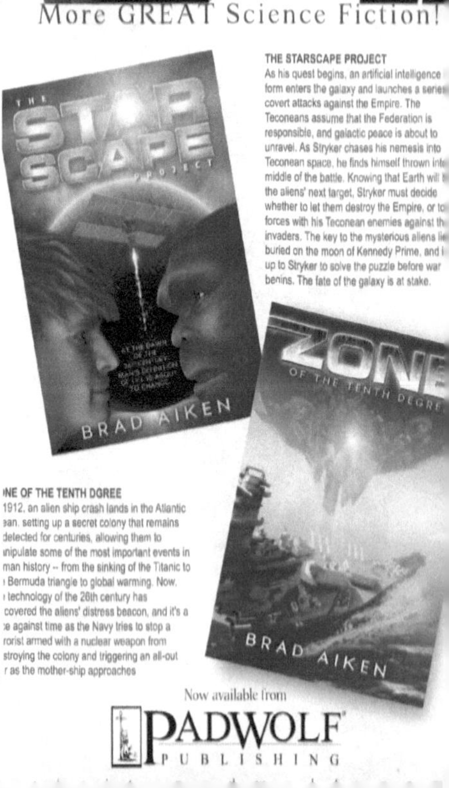
More GREAT Science Fiction!
THE STARSCAPE PROJECT
As his quest begins, an artificial intelligence form enters the galaxy and launches a series covert attacks against the Empire. The Teconeans assume that the Federation is responsible, and galactic peace is about to unravel. As Stryker chases his nemesis into Teconean space, he finds himself thrown into middle of the battle. Knowing that Earth will be the aliens' next target, Stryker must decide whether to let them destroy the Empire, or to forces with his Teconean enemies against the invaders. The key to the mysterious aliens lie buried on the moon of Kennedy Prime, and i up to Stryker to solve the puzzle before war begins. The fate of the galaxy is at stake.
THE STAR SCAPE PROJECT
BRAD AIKEN
ZONE OF THE TENTH DEGREE
BRAD AIKEN
NE OF THE TENTH DGREE
1912, an alien ship crash lands in the Atlantic ean, setting up a secret colony that remains detected for centuries, allowing them to nipulate some of the most important events in man history -- from the sinking of the Titanic to Bermuda triangle to global warming. Now, technology of the 26th century has covered the aliens' distress beacon, and it's a e against time as the Navy tries to stop a rorist armed with a nuclear weapon from stroying the colony and triggering an all-out r as the mother-ship approaches
Now available from
PADWOLF
PUBLISHING

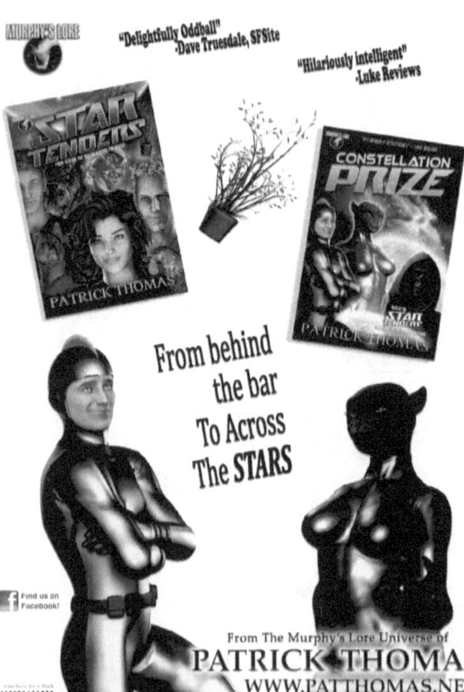

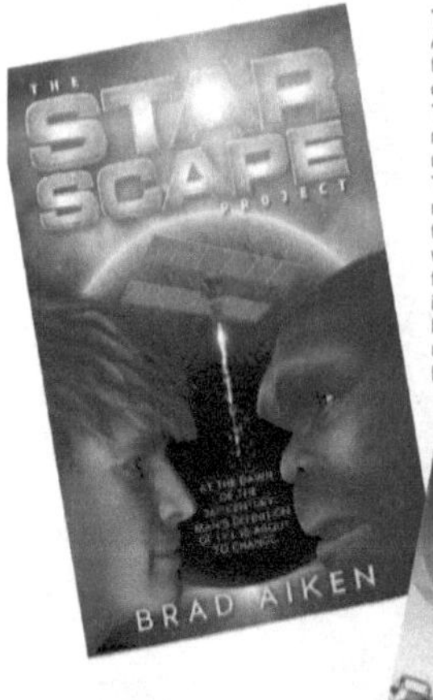

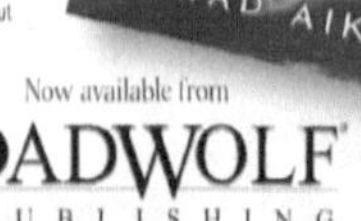

DOWN THESE MEANS STREETS

of Magic & Monsters walk the

MYSTIC INVESTIGATORS

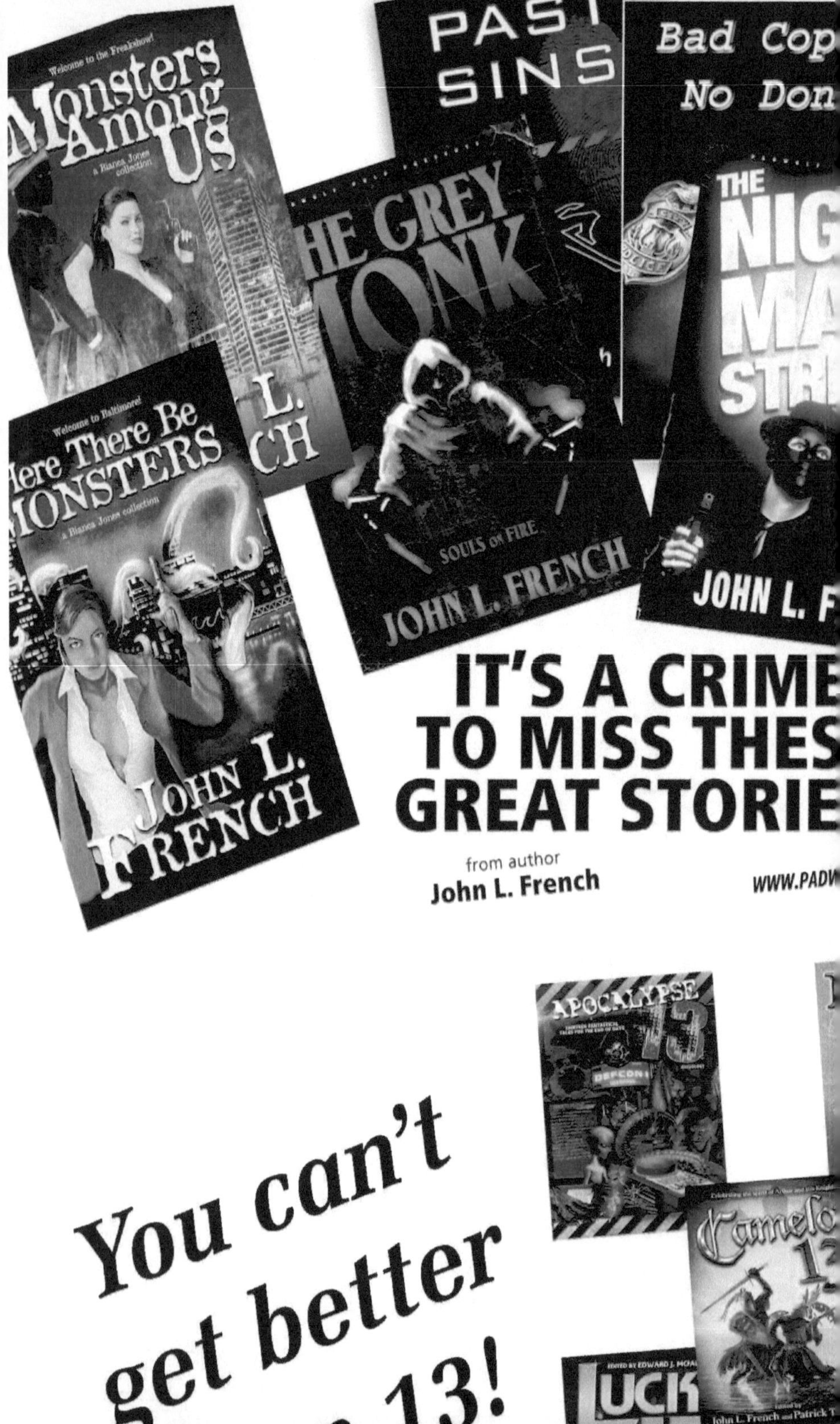
Welcome to the Freakshow!
Monsters Among Us
a Bianca Jones collection

PAST SINS

Bad Cop
No Don

THE GREY MONK
SOULS ON FIRE
JOHN L. FRENCH

THE NIGHT MA STR

Welcome to Baltimore!
Here There Be MONSTERS
a Bianca Jones collection
JOHN L. FRENCH

JOHN L. FRENCH

JOHN L. F

IT'S A CRIME
TO MISS THES
GREAT STORIE
from author
John L. French
WWW.PADW

APOCALYPSE 13
THIRTEEN FANTASTICAL
TALES FOR THE END OF DAYS
DEFCON 1

Camelo

EDITED BY EDWARD J. MOA
LUCK
John L. French and Patrick T

You can't get better 13!

Sometimes it takes a monster to keep the Abyss at bay.

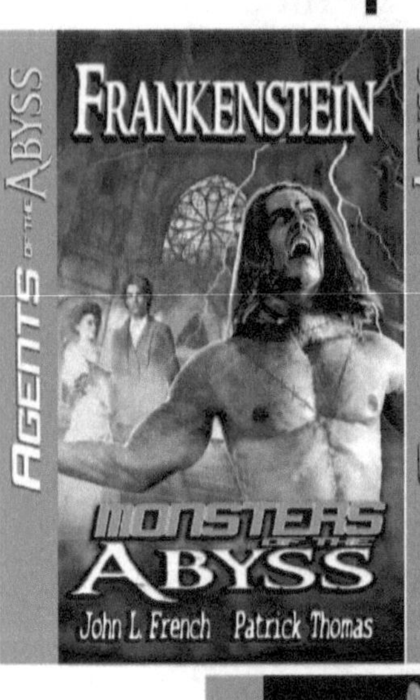